I0571578

LOGOS

Second Edition, Paperback – published 2010
Twisted Knickers Publications

This book is a work of fiction. References to real people, events, establishments,
organizations, or locales are intended only to provide a sense of authenticity,
and are used fictitiously. All other characters, and all incidents and dialogue,
are drawn from the author's imagination and are not construed as real. Attribu-
tion for public domain works and quotations included within the text are noted
as necessary.

ISBN: 978-0-9822145-2-7

Printed in the USA

Cover and Interior Image Editing and Design provided by Twisted Knickers
Imaging Services. Cover Image and Detail: *The Last Judgment* by Jan Van Eyck
ca. 1430, The Met Museum, NYC, NY Public Domain Photographic Image provided by Wikimedia Commons. Verse in Chapters 5 and 13: The Egyptian Book
of the Dead, E. A. Wallis Budge, translation [1895].

In all chaos there is a cosmos,
In all disorder, a secret order.
Carl Jung

CHERYL ANNE GARDNER

L⊕G⊕S

A
TWISTED KNICKERS PUBLICATION

1

Proem

T he first I witnessed blood shed condemned my soul to the darkness. The first I shed that of another sealed my fate, and the first I gave of my own set me free.

Imagine, if you will, a you that eternity could never possibly comprehend. Imagine yourself a creature immune to time and its intrigues, a ghoulish creature, a devil, a fiend, borne of rot and hatred. A slave to death, imprisoned by walls of flesh and bone, of sex and sinew, yet at the core of your existence you are but a shadow, and for all your ferocity, what remains of the spring ephemeral you once knew as your spirit is now nothing more than the tainted reflection of an infinite, abysmal darkness—all light forsaken, all vows wretched, and all desire wanton. Now imagine the cold isolation you might feel, and when the chill of it hits the marrow of your bones then you will understand that *that* is the life of a ShadowLeiche, my life, such as it was: desolate, devoid of sentiment and any shred of emotional intimacy. Nevertheless, I have had a long time to ponder my predicament, so I have grown accustomed to the darkness. Have been affected by it in the sense that I have acquired a morose affinity for it. Its thin veil of calm conceals the distance between who I was and what I am. It conceals my anger and my pain, and it conceals the merciless wrath that I have set loose indiscriminately upon the world for centuries.

I am manifest destiny. I am malice and deceit. I am refusal, I am arrogance, and I can slice open your heart and gut your soul. Resistance is ignorant futility. I can see everything, can know everything. All that you hold dear is laid bare before me, and I can wound you to the very core of your being, strip you of your flesh, and turn all of your deepest, darkest thoughts and desires against you until shame, humiliation, and guilt consume you. I am an influence peddler—the unrepentant voice of hopelessness and depravity—whispering a medley of irresistible persuasions into your ear.

With no more than a casual glance over my shoulder, I can see the past, the future, and all of the infinite possibilities in between. I *am* infinite—observer, juror—and I *am* judgment, its edict wielded with menacing force, sheathed in the slick conviction of twilight's armor. My father had given me a name once, a name lost to me now. All I know of my own soul is the hatred that cast me into the abyss. Emissary of chaos, agent of disorder, or cosmic executioner, whatever you choose to call me, I can command the powers of the elements with an incidental thought, and I can curse forth a thousand unimaginable plagues. I am the will…I am the way…I am the bitter end of existence, and I can tear your soul apart. My name is Selena…I *am* the sword in the shadows.

Yes, the mere thought of my existence may be difficult for the mind to accept. Mortals don't really want to know what stirs in the dark, let alone look it in the eye. They fear the wolf come at night clawing at the door. They whimper and tremble when they hear the raven's wings beating against the shutters like the wind in the gloaming. Yes, they can feel death, can feel the cold steel edging against their spines—always. Every new moon brings no merit beyond the shadows. So no, mortals just don't have the courage or the fortitude for such a leap of faith. They use ignorance as a shield, believing that denial will protect them in some way.

It won't, not from me, and I am not the only monster you need fear in the dark. Many supernatural creatures wander the dimly lit places of this putrid world. Unfortunately, provision had long ago been created for the lot of us, and so the Leiche are oftentimes mistaken for other more notorious immortals. We *may* share some insignificant similarities with our brethren—although we do have better table manners—but that is as far as it goes. Beyond death we are, more or less—immortal—beyond redemption, or so it has long been written. Souls lost to the darkness the scriptures claim: a morbid affliction upon the earth.

But it's all lies, you see. All lies.

Our paths crossed the darkness, very deliberately so, and we, by choice, embraced it, forsaking all we thought we knew in our mortal ignorance. I can see things you'll never see. I can know truth, the truth that divinity often obscures. I knew I had not been cast out of Eden, and so I searched: for answers, for others. But no matter how long and how deeply I pursued the knowledge I felt was my birth-right, the ancient religious texts—old folktales and myths to me now—never clearly defined by what mystical means we do or do not endure our own births and deaths. How the Leiche came to be, how I came to be, was forbidden knowledge hidden in linguistic vagaries too opaque to translate, and so all I found was endless crumbling pages, fragmented philosophies, and poetic words. I found no enlightenment. The answers I sought until now had eluded me, leaving me only with more equally irritating questions. What's more, in over two thousand years of pointless wandering, I had never met another of my own kind. There was no one to beseech in the darkness. Even the so-called metaphysical scholars were of no use, and the alchemists, who reached with their will into the seething depths of magic and mysticism, found nothing there but allusion. No one possessed the answers to that mystery—the mystery of my existence. No one. And in time, I convinced myself that I was utterly alone in my misery, existing on the outer reaches of divinity, no more than another grotesquery among many. Yes, many were the loathsome creatures that lived at my side in the darkness. Vile creatures that had infiltrated every corner of the world. We all know the legends; know them as if the abominations had cradled us at birth themselves.

Vampires—wretched bloodsuckers—are, beyond all doubt, the most disgusting of the beasts, no better than pathetic mortals with rabies. A pack of flea-bitten mangy dogs, barking at the moon's waxing glow. They kill for their own pleasure and gluttony, and it makes me sick, but alas, they do pretend to have codes of honor: what they would consider ethics. The term ethics by their definition *is* a stretch of the imagination. To me, it's all badly tailored justifications really, and so as you might expect, they always fall just short of grace with their false mimicry. Divine they are not. Gods they are not. They are simply sad little marionettes dancing in contorted spasms from filaments of frayed twine, and reapers —the cloaked moody ones—well, they are merely automatons doing their duty: ticket takers, nothing more. The Lycanthropes have more personality, but this story is not about the beasts.

The Leiche are not death dealers in that sense. We are not angels or demons either. Angels and demons labor for the Gods—each on their chosen side be it good or evil— punishing mortals, as they are charged to do. It's all about divine retribution for them, no matter how you look at it. The righteous suffer and the evil-doers suffer. I have never seen a soul saved through suffering, have never witnessed a divine epiphany spring forth from the lament of the languishing, so I have always held fast to the belief that the Leiche uphold a more otherworldly purpose. Sometimes you just have to have faith in that which you cannot explain, and sometimes, you just have to do what you are told to do. We work for the greater anarchy of the Universe. We answer to no one, and it doesn't have to make sense. We are the harnessers of souls, and we will drag you kicking and screaming into the light if we must. Blades gleaming fiercely in the cold cutting shimmer of the moon, we *are* the dark horsemen mounted proudly upon our pale steeds. Our purpose is inevitable. Our actions—instinctual. We have no conscience with which to do battle, no ethical aspirations to taint our reason. We are not vigilantes for the greater good of humanity, either. There is neither right nor wrong within the grand scheme of things.

Salvation of the spirit. That is all that matters, and chaos has always been the vehicle of deliverance.

Revelations 6:8 states that we, the Leiche and our brethren, had been given sovereignty over a fourth of the earth: To Kill with Sword, To Kill with Famine and with Pestilence, and To Kill by Wild Beasts.

The innocent perish just as the wicked. God doesn't discriminate, and neither do I. I have taken my share of each, have gnawed on the bones with little remorse or regret. Pity? Forgiveness? Dross sentiments, nothing more. It is not in our nature to nurture such ill-advised ideals. We have no right to feel compassion; never have had, not since the dawning of time. Deliverance calls for cold neutrality. A sympathetic will is a weakened will and of no use to anyone.

Terse sentiments aside, I would be most willing to share some of my stories with you—a little morbid vignette or two to tantalize the spirit—and depending on your particular threshold for such things, these stories might just rot your flesh from the bone, that is, if you can stand to hear them or even begin to understand them. You might even question the divide between hell and heaven. Be there no God greater than sacrificial will, be there no Eden as delightful as death. Plato once said, 'No one knows whether death, which people fear to be the greatest evil, may not be the greatest good.'

I will let you decide for yourself. I have faced my own death a thousand times over. I have no opinion to offer you; consolation is not mine to give.

However, allow me to start at the beginning with the blazing glory of the Roman Empire: a boiling cauldron frothing over with the worst of human tyranny and decadence.

It was the beginning…

The beginning and the end of my mortal life.

2

A Child ... *A Prisoner of Rome*

I n 12 BC, Nero Claudius Drusus, tormented by a malignancy of the spirit and intent on establishing Roman control in Germania, crossed the mighty Rhenus with dread purpose and darkness' legion at his back. They moved with the mist, long-stridden over rock, field, wood, and stream, and despite the ardor and bravery of my people, the slaughter was far beyond reason or measure.

I remember the flames, the acrid stench of scorched flesh, and the screams, deadened by the horses' hooves pounding against the damp soil. I remember running, hiding, and then running again, and then I remember everything slipping from my grasp, everything except for the laughter—callous, sinister laughter. Life, for me, had fallen upon a blunt edge. The darkness had descended, thick and viscous like the mud in my hair, and I could still hear the laughter…and the wind, whispering my name.

The siege lasted many months, and amid the chaos, I watched in silence and in fear as the Roman tyrants drank the blood of our heroes, raped and bludgeoned the innocent souls of our women, and burned our homes to the ground. Many Germanic tribes were either subjugated or obliterated, and by 9 BC, Nero's militia had torn a chasm into the earth, pushing the boundary of northern Roman Germania all the way to the blood-soaked banks of the Albis.

A casualty of war at thirteen years old—a child—a prisoner—condemned to a life of servitude in Rome.

This was the fate that the Gods had chosen for me.

It is far easier to break the will of a mighty warrior than it is to break that of a child, so I pushed all traces of memory from my mind: the time endless journey, the ragged clothes, the starvation of my body…my broken bones and my ravaged flesh. I even renounced the lament of my soul, but I would never forget Rome.

Rome, the city of my destruction, my awakening: the city of my rebirth.

My misery had not begun there and would certainly not end there, but it was the root of my suffering, the justification for my apathetic point of view, and much later, it would become the impetus for my infernal desire for destruction. Its intrusiveness was affecting, of course. One felt defeated almost instantly by its presence, but to me, Rome was more than monolithic stone temples and aqueducts. Yes, its sheer magnitude was awe inspiring, its beauty almost ghastly in its defiance. It was so frighteningly different from the sprawling marshlands of my youth that for the first time in my life, I actually felt small, but what struck me more than Rome's lofty presence were the Romans themselves. I could not fathom that humans were capable of such monumental acts of concordance, such belligerent refutations of vulgarity, and yet, in appalling contrast, would be so willing to enthrall themselves with the clandestine embracement of vile atrocities and intrigues. The balance between vice and virtue was as precarious as a Caesar's temperament —volatile and always a breath away from the edge.

The streets were much the same.

The odors and the echoes of the city combined to create a ubiquitous din. The distilled essence of smoked meats, herbs and spices, perfumed oils, and the soft scent of linen and silk saturated even the minutest particles of dust floating throughout the seething mass of cackling and screaming merchants. From every conceivable direction, one could be assured of an assault on their senses. At any given time of the day, there were so many people hustling and bustling at the markets and auctions that it was utter bedlam. Disagreements, accusations…amicable arrangements, and the ever-present allure of sobbing and begging were attractions worth the price of admission. The streets ran afoul with blood, urine, and the fermenting juices of overripe fruit crushed under careless foot. The desire to vomit or swoon was ever a footfall away. One could go mad from the suffocating closeness of it all.

As I wandered from merchant to merchant, I tried not to think of my imprisonment, because no matter how filthy and base the streets seemed to me, I could always look up at the sky. So often was I found staring into the evening sky, wanting for the moon's sickly embrace, that when a name was chosen for me, it was agreed that my soul would forever belong to the dark of that waning moon. *Selene* they called me: Greek Goddess of the moon, slave to the night sky. Yes, it was a worthy name for a soul cast into darkness, and in that darkness, among the shifting shadows, I could make my escape: there I could fly. I imagined often that the light of the moon was the same flickering and tremulous luminescence that lay across the mountains and the moors of my homeland. For that nostalgic imagining, I would readily take being accosted and degraded on the street over housebound servitude. Truth be told, I actually loved the manic disorder of it all. Order always seemed in violent flux, and I, apparently, possessed an almost suicidal inclination towards the chaotic. So when I could—while taking care of household tasks charged to me by the affluent family who held my service—I spent much of my time ambling about those streets. Yes, I had been auctioned off as a slave, but a child slave fares far better, and my situation was no exception.

Nothing derogatory could be said of my masters. Kind-hearted people they were—generous—and they cared for me as much like a daughter as they were able. It was as worthy a life as any slave could hope to have, and the only pain I ever suffered was of that inside my heart. I missed my family, and the torturous memory of their deaths poisoned any affection that I might have ever felt for my surrogates. I never wept or felt shameful of my hatred of them, even though I probably should have. My hatred was far reaching, but it wasn't their fault really. In upholding the tedious status quo, they were simply perpetuating an age-old doctrine yet unwritten. Man's perceived dominion over the lesser lay at the heart of all human treachery. The great sickness of humanity, I called it, and as for love, even if there existed such a thing in my world, consequence had rendered me incapable. One might have better fortune letting blood from a stone.

I never felt the need to reconcile my emotions—they were what they were—and I allowed myself to feel them and express them in all their erratic complexity. All that had been good in me had died, and I had accepted it. What choice did I have?

My life was uneventful for several years. I knew compassion, pity, and generosity. Even without love, I lived well and privileged, and my education was far superior to what most slaves would have received—that being none. Consent to my desire for an education came without protest. My arguments were grounded in sycophantic logic. They knew this, and my irritating and aggressive doggedness about the subject overruled any reservations they might have had. An educated slave would indeed improve the standing of the household, so even though the lady of the house mock-scolded the settlement at me with hands clenched into fists against her hips, the acquiescence was not philanthropy on their part, I assure you.

I must admit that my innate longing for knowledge of all varieties was savage in its hunger—shameless and savage. Sometimes I felt that the longing was the only thing keeping me alive. My need to know *why* fuelled my every breath. Why had my life been spared? No act of mercy could be so paradoxical: spare me death to make me a slave, devalue me, and make a mockery of my existence. This contradiction tasted of acid in my throat. That cynicism was the deep-seated nature of my longing, so I refused to let myself stoop to irrational thought, or worse, allow myself to fall prey to ignorance, to consider my predicament as charity, or to count my own blessings. No. I would never concede to a life of delusional contentment for that would be a slower more agonizing death. My soul was not indigent, and I would never allow it to suffer impoverishment of that magnitude.

When I was permitted to speak, which was a rare occurrence, I could hold no commonplace discussion without setting off down a path of philosophical obscurity. The relentless barrage of questions I assailed them with was infinite, and my tactical approach was akin to a bloody mêlée. Even if they understood the questions and had any worthwhile answers to offer up, they wouldn't have been given a moment's breath to speak out. To take a familial tone with me would have been unacceptable. It wasn't worth the risk, even if they wanted or needed to comfort me, and so my masters, due to circumstantial guilt, did not take my fanaticism for belligerence. They saw it as more of a nervous behavioral tic, and while severe punishment would have been the norm for speaking out in such a way, the only remedy they could think of that might exhaust me would require numerous tutors and hefty fees as payment for their knowledge and their discretion.

The tutors arrived in the multitudes.

After a time, order and some semblance of sanity

were restored to the household, and I found a renewed interest in my duties. Feed the hunger, keep the demon at bay. Seemed logical, and it worked for a while, but the rules of logic are often misinterpreted. To me, logic was just another form of bondage, one to be risen above, and through the tutors, I had discovered that the word could set me free. In poetry, anything is possible.

You see, the Age of Augustus, later called the Golden Era of Roman Literature, offered copious amounts of intellectual fodder for any whom desired the wisdom. There were many poets, and of the three greatest at that time: Horace, Virgil, and Ovid, it was Virgil who I professed as my muse. *The Aenid* is an epic poem, glorifying the heroic greatness of Rome. This greatness, however it seemed to permeate every fiber of my life, was not what absorbed me so profoundly. What held my heart and mind in suspended animation was the Stoic philosophy imbued throughout its text—a philosophy which held that the Universe was deliberately patterned, and within that complex pattern of mystery, truth, and lies, there existed a secret balance between order and chaos. This balance had a larger purpose and meaning, so the Stoics called it logos, and it was believed that this *Logos* originated in the divine mind of the Universe.

It didn't take logic to convince myself that all the answers I sought could be found in the Logos, answers that would release me from my bonds, and this idea of freedom drilled deeply into my psyche. So deeply that it became an obsession, one in which I had significant difficulty controlling. What did it mean to be free? The mind was a prisoner of logic, the heart a prisoner of faith, and the soul, a prisoner of the flesh. There seemed only one true path to freedom, and the thought of it gnawed at my soul like the itch of festering wound. I could not control my urge to tear at its ragged flesh, could not resist worrying it until my fingers were bloodied.

My masters also shared my frustration, in that they had great difficulty controlling me. Up to this point, I had been spared the rod, but into each life there cometh the pain that spurs us on.

As the blossom of womanhood took hold of my body, a kinetic energy began to surge within, through, and all around me as if a thousand tiny pins were stabbing at my sanity. I espied strange creatures everywhere in the darkness, lurking and whispering insidious plots, and on my eighteenth birthday, the flashes began—short circuits in the static of my brain. The pain was so intense that I often fainted, even in front of guests.

Promptly, I was rushed away for medical attention, but the physicians were baffled. They had no insight as to what afflicted me. Some were convinced that I was possessed of evil spirits, as I would babble hysterically, describing in horrific detail the numerous grisly visions that had invaded my mind without reprieve: fornication, rape, murder, torture, and death. I dreamt drifts of barren land engulfed in flames rising up under my charred and blistered feet, and I dreamt of blood-soaked, mangled bodies, strewn beyond the scorched horizon, bodies reaching out to me—twisting and flexing their entangled sinews maliciously throughout my consciousness—as the wind swept the flames into my hair and carried the lament of the dying to the heavens like a soft whispering. *Whispering.* There was always the incessant whispering …and screaming. It was the screaming that drove me mad. Mad enough to mutilate myself and beg for death, and yet despite this, fortune would again forsake me.

I didn't take long before my masters reached the limit of what they could abide: a mad slave was not only an inconvenience but was also an embarrassment that could not be tolerated in such prestigious circles of society. Even so, the only course of action they saw fit to take, unlike their fellow slave owners, was one of compassion. They had the money and the status to stay my execution, and so I was to be exiled to the Vestal Temple with hope that the Goddess would cure me and restore me to innocence and obedience.

That was not to be the case.

Two years of endless incantations, bloodletting, incense, and bitter draughts of anti-psychotic herbal mixtures passed to no avail. Through spasms, screams, and prayers, my voice reached to the heavens and fell back to blackened depths unanswered, but I kept praying and pleading for my salvation anyway.

In due course, the pain subsided somewhat, and the images coagulating in my mind became more cohesive and controlled. I discovered that I held dominion over my own fate. I had not been granted that power; the Logos had not answered my pleas for mercy. No. That power had to come from within, and I came to realize that it had always been mine—mine to wield as I saw fit. I found that I could push my thoughts into the minds of others, could cross the threshold into the dream state and transform their fanciful visions into nightmares. I could see through the past and into the future, and I foretold of many terrible events.

A Pythia had arisen in their midst it seemed, and the

Temple virgins became extremely frightened of me.

My purgatory had become their torment.

My ablution had become their blood.

Their fear fed my anger, but more importantly, it fed something else that was growing inside of me. Something shapeless, and nameless, and faceless. Something devoid of morality and thereby free from its bonds.

With each new moon that passed, my power increased exponentially. I didn't know what I could do, and what I couldn't, but nothing seemed beyond my control or beyond being affected by my emotions. In time, I was able to move objects with a thought and call upon the elements for my own amusement.

I could no longer remember my birth name. The last remaining remnants of my innocence had finally been consumed by that dread moon, so I counted the comets streaking across the sky, I cleansed my soul in stardust, and eventually, I forgave myself my anger.

During the last of many purgings, I sealed the wound as quickly as the blade released my skin, and I set the priestess to burn. Whips of Vestal Flame lashed at her flesh under the command of my will…and I laughed. I laughed at her pain. She, with the long flowing hair and the taint of innocence upon her lips, she who had put herself above me and had condemned me as a sinner. Yes, I laughed at her. Doubled over in ecstasy, I laughed as the sin of her own soul was charred to cinders.

It was my twentieth birthday and the last day I would spend in the Temple of Vesta.

3

Sanctuary

⎯⎯⎯⎯⎯⎯⎯⎯⎯⎯⎯⎯⎯⎯⎯⎯⎯⎯⎯⎯⎯⎯⎯⎯⎯⎯⎯

Brothels, though rarely discussed in polite society beyond a whisper, were a source of employment for many a woman in Rome's vast empire. Cast out of the Temple, there was no escaping the street, and I had nowhere else to turn for refuge.

Rumors travel upon swift breezes. It was said that I had been branded a bad omen, but the Vestals feared me too much to accuse me of magic or slaughter me outright. I had taken command of the Vestal Flame, and that was something to be feared. Fear is a powerful motivator. I could have probably walked out of Rome with my head held high. Yes, I could have done that; however, Rome was all I knew of life, and compared to the abuses I had endured, the brothel seemed as comfortable a refuge as any other. Sanctuary is a place rarely known to a slave, so it's not to one's advantage to be too particular.

In the months that passed, I fared far better than I had expected. My Germanic features, flaxen hair, and lithe voluptuous body transformed me, rather quickly, into the most sought after service maiden in the city. I am sure my *charm* had something to do with it as well: the ability to personify another's need is a rare talent. I eventually held status among the elite few who were endowed with the ability to choose their own clientele. I, myself, favored the austere military man, as their brute force served only to arouse my playful side. I tormented their minds and bodies with such intensity that many took a fortnight or more to rest and recuperate, and yet, they always came back, begging for more.

Fate had landed me in an oasis in the midst of the squalor. I had discovered myself not lost but found. I also found myself showered with gold and jewels, more riches than I could ever have aspired to spend, and this good fortune was not lost on me, for it afforded me time —time for myself—to read, learn, and take delight in the lovely garden that surrounded the brothel and the baths. You see, this was the most respected brothel in the city, its walls ornamented with priceless artistic masterpieces, depicting, of course, the menu of licentious pleasures that could be entertained for a price. We were courtesans, almost royalty, and the men—well-travelled aristocrats and high-ranking soldiers—brought me all manner of gifts from faraway lands: poetry, plays, philosophy, al-chemy, and enchantments too numerous to mention in one breath. And I devoured everything. From the latest fashion to the transgressive, I licked every last delectable word from the pages. These *men*, they paid me in secrets, and I earned their trust with discretion. That's what they bought and paid for: intimacy without complication or complaint, and they paid well.

In return for their generosity, a multitude of possible futures I divined for their choosing. If they desired love, then I professed my undying devotion. If they desired subjugation, I fell humbled at their command, and if they desired debasement, then I whipped their flesh raw. No matter their craving, they all left my embrace satisfied with what they perceived to have taken from me, which was very amusing to say the least, since I felt as though I had given absolutely nothing in return. As they thrashed wildly about, sweating and grunting and thrusting like animals in the throes of bestial desire, I never dispensed with nor suffered one single emotion.

Only a fool could possibly mistake contempt for passion, and I have lain prostrate under many a fool. Let them be damned as fools. It mattered little what vile supplications were demanded of my flesh, I simply consumed their energy—rejuvenating myself—fortifying the power that coursed angrily within me. Although I rose to the occasion and adequately performed my part in the nightly satirical farce, I cared not for any of them...not until Lucius. Lovely Lucius, blessed with the unearthly beauty of Adonis. The day I met Lucius was the day I discovered love and just how treacherous it could be.

That day was a fine day amid my twenty-fifth year, a cloudless day, and the city was buzzing with the return of soldiers from Alexandria. Thousands upon thousands of flower petals scented of virginal innocence dusted the

streets. They swirled in the air, whirled, twirled and un-
dulated with the breath of the crowd, until finally, they
fell back to the earth, settling between the bare feet of the
wailing and swooning young women who had flooded
the docks at their fathers' command to pay homage to
Rome's warrior class.

Anyone who lived within the reach of the Roman
Empire at that time had heard the ancient victory tale of
Julius Caesar's capturing of Alexandria, and they would
have also heard the tragic elegy of Cleopatra's suicide.

Always great are the tales of triumph and misery.
Passed down from generation to generation, no written
word was ever needed, for tales of conquest are forever
embedded in the soul of a soldier. I knew the history of
Alexandria all too well. I felt Rome's venom surge
through Cleopatra's breast as if the asp were entwined
with my own soul. I could feel the city burn, could feel
the flames licking at my mind with every soldier's
heated breath against my lips.

Suffering the loss of their beloved Cleopatra, along
with the subsequent bitter defeat of the once mighty
Ptolemaic navy at Actium, the mighty Greek city of
Alexandria had fallen to ruin under the malefic rule of
Julius Caesar and then later Augustus.

Over the years, military garrisons stationed in Alexandria maintained a tenuous peace while keeping a
fervent watch over the Alexandrian Mob, which Roman
rule with all its power, control, and intrigues had not
managed to weaken. So feared it was, so deeply rooted,
it would continue to thrive and prosper under Roman
dominion, and Rome spared no expense in its vigil to
appease it, which was a boon for women of my stature

and profession: the supply of military men, diplomats, and Praetorian guards seeking distraction was an endless wellspring of fortune.

As I stood on the balcony that day, the wind carelessly tussling the braids of my hair, I shielded my eyes from the sun and watched the ships rock gently against the sea as a flood of service-worn soldiers, officers, and guards spilled out into the city. That sea glistened in the sunlight as if it were an agitated mass of silver-leaf-coated glass. I wished upon that bejeweled sea often, hoping that one day it would whisk me away, drown me, or bring forth my salvation, and each idle, ill-conceived wish I cast away upon its waters took with it a piece of my soul.

I closed my eyes, bit into my lip, and wished again.

When I opened my eyes, I felt a heady lightness of limb, as if I were intoxicated. Among those returning, a brutally handsome guard captured my wild eye. His bawdy comrades were harassing him in the street, elbowing and nudging him towards the brothel, trying to persuade him that this very den of iniquity was indeed the place to seek relief for his travel weary senses.

While watching the scuffle, a grave impression overcame me. His manner seemed off. He seemed almost shy in a way. As he slowly shuffled towards the portico, his lowered eyes and the slouch in his shoulders indicated that the decision to concede to the whims of his comrades had inflamed an old wound—a wound that, for a moment, seemed to equal the torment of my own.

I couldn't take my eyes off him. I watched as his foot, hesitant, stopped him at the steps. Perhaps his will had faltered at the prospect of what he was about to do,

but a reprieve from whatever he was struggling with
was not to be found in the pebbles or the dust he shifted
aimlessly about with his feet. Was it guilt? It couldn't be.
There was no shame here, no shame in a man taking
what he needed *or* what he felt compelled to take for
sheer pleasure's sake. No man could possibly feel shame
for that, so I didn't know why he looked up from his
feet. I didn't know for sure if he felt my gaze upon him,
or if he simply felt the intense desire and attraction held
within it, but it didn't really matter: he looked up—not to
seek console in the breeze or remedy from the cloudless
sky—he looked up at me.

I tried to ignore the flush I felt in my veins, and so
with a cavalier yet inviting wave of my hand, I beckoned
to him. He acknowledged my invitation with glance cast
awkwardly aside and a slight almost tortured smile. An
innocent smile. Innocence I wanted to partake of greedily
in an effort to regain some in return. As I fell over myself
running to meet him, I imagined him waiting, desperate,
arms open, and my leaping into them, then a smile and a
passionate kiss before the Gods whisked us away to
another land, a better land. It took only a moment to fall
back down from the clouds, realizing I had succumbed
to a worthless fantasy. My heart had never desired anything before, and, even if it had, I had always dismissed
it as nothing more than fanciful thoughts, so always the
consummate professional, I discarded those absurd
thoughts like so much worn out bombast. When I met
him at the portico, I took his hand in mine and gently
led him into one of the lavishly adorned service rooms.

As the room opened up around us and the tormented
echoes of the darkened corridor faded into the distance,

I heard his breath catch in his throat with a gasp as if he had never seen sex adorned with such splendor before. He stood perfectly still, squeezing my hand as he stared down at the spectacular mosaics covering the floors, as he glanced in awe at the frescoed marble slabs lining the walls, and as he threw his head back in wonderment to appreciate the ivory and gold ornamentation covering the ceiling's bare exposed beams. Even though I had grown accustomed to my surroundings, admittedly, it was impressive. A rich, sensual retreat it was indeed: fit for a God, let alone a mortal man. But even the sumptuous comforts could not spare him from being overcome by uneasiness, and neither would I.

Illuminated by the intense glow of the fire, I turned him around to face me so that I could afford myself a moment to better scrutinize him. He released my hand and backed away a step. He looked ordinary for a guard of his obvious level. Clad in his uniform, he had an air of imposing authority about him, despite the fidgeting as he idly shifted his feet and adjusted the sword at his side for no real reason. He was lovely, yes, that was the word. So lovely. His tanned skin and sharp features favored the long, dark, lustrous hair that tumbled unfettered and mischievous over his forehead and into his hard blue eyes. Eyes of a liquid blue, flecked with amber and mahogany — and they shone, like mirrors in the fire's wicked blaze as a wild beast's would in the light of the full moon.

With respect, I allowed him the customary distance and silence until the monetary portion of our exchange was dispensed with. It's a delicate thing: intimacy, especially when it has a price. So what struck more than his shyness was that he seemed unaffected when he tossed the heavy purse at my feet. Normally I would have counted it at least. Expectation dictates payment. That's the *need*, and I don't like speculation, but this time, I just kicked the purse away. His indifference to my gesture filled me with delight, and I felt wild with impatience, which was altogether contradictory to my nature. I actually *wanted* him. It was the first time in my life I had ever wanted anything, so I advanced towards him, deliberately and intimately, while allowing my robes to drop to the floor, at which point, he averted his gaze from my flesh and backed even farther away from me.

"No," he whispered with a hint of trivial shyness, and while I respected the rejection, it had me piqued enough to retort with a questioning: My Lord? and a gentle reminder that he had paid, *generously*. He didn't seem to notice the sour riposte and responded back with an almost ludicrous justification, to which I countered with a bit of well-deserved sarcasm: "Abstinence my Lord," I declared. "Well, I *have* heard of such a thing. How *very* noble of you." But my overt and impolite interruption made no difference. Unmoved, he resumed with his eyes to the floor. "Not really, no," he said with a self-deprecating altruism I was certain was not his own. "It is true that I paid, yes, but not for what you…not for what one might expect from a…I only wish to speak with you. Forgive my words. I am weary from my travels, and your beauty, such subtle and innocent beauty, it confuses and overwhelms me."

My taste for men had always leant more towards simple and hearty fare, a bit of bread and water, enough to satisfy, but this one—a shy soldier, stoic, and yet adept at flattery—this man was manifest contradiction.

He wasn't an ordinary man at all, and I could already feel the heat upon my lips. I couldn't help but swoon as I seated myself next to him—unsure that I should have—and yet, without due consideration, I felt compelled to touch and caress his trembling leg. And so I did, but I felt distant, from my actions and from my own words. "And what would the topic be, my Lord?" I asked without any real concern for the answer before continuing with the *always* effective self-serving and self-deprecating: I am well educated in many things, in spite of my line of work statement. I didn't need to say it, obviously. Everything in my life was in spite of something, but I was certain I could find a neutral topic to satisfy his need for conversation. "Something to ease your *pain*, perhaps, my Lord."

With that, he shifted inward, leaning into my solicitous tack, or so I had assumed, but then, he crossed the room, lifted my robes from the floor and returned to cover my bare skin—his reticence overruling my audacity. I wasn't at all prepared when he declared that *love* was the subject he wished to discuss. He said the word so plainly, as if his soul were smiling with haughty delight at the outward simplicity of it.

Of course, I knew better. There was nothing simple about the word, let alone the motivations that defined it. I clenched my robes and pulled them tighter to my body, and without sounding disrespectful, my admission was as candid as I could make it. "Well, my Lord, of that I know very little. I'm sorry for being abrupt; please, allow me to explain: You see, love is completely worthless, and it is an intolerable disadvantage for someone of my obvious means. I have never known love, cannot know love. It is a possibility I have never considered. It is an idea fraught with futility, and it warrants no merit. I cannot embrace it if I am to survive."

He smiled in agreement, eyes glistening in the fire-light; then his face lost all expression, and his chin fell towards his chest as he nodded out his reply, "I feared as much, and, in that, my lady, we are alike. But I thought, well...I thought we might attempt to discover it together ...that is, if you would willingly suffer my company?"

He punctuated that question with a rather earnest look cast directly into my eyes, and as his gaze deepened into mine, I noted a trace of sadness. Washed in black, it seemed a remnant of regret, the last vestige of some ter-rible anguish—old and decrepit—suffered an eternity ago. This was no ruse to lure me into his impoverished clutches. He held his sincerity close, his pain even closer. I wanted to comfort him—a want so completely foreign to me that it set me entirely off balance.

I felt weak. I felt powerless, drowning in the oceans of blue that flooded his eyes. I felt a blush of unexpected warmth move over me. I could not recall ever gazing upon such a gentle face, could not recall such kindness ever in the whole of my life. And although his request was quite unnerving, it was all the more compelling. So even before my mind could resolve one thousand and one excuses, I graciously accepted his offer.

I reached out, slid my hand into his, and let myself fall.

4

A Slave to Love ... *A Slave to Hatred*

Alexander The Great, in an effort to expand the boundaries of his own growing empire, had adopted an aggressive and unconventional attitude when it came to integrating foreigners into his administration and his army. This, of course, led historians and scholars to credit him with *a policy of fusion*, albeit a twisted one, for his steadfast belief in divine conquest kept him always precariously poised between acts of terrorism and heroic diplomacy. He so readily embraced this desire for assimilation, or unification as he chose to see it, that he encouraged marriage between his army and foreigners and practiced it on numerous occasions himself as well.

Not that this history mattered to any great degree in the moments we spent together, but it was something Lucius and I shared. We were both borne of subjugation, assimilation, and chaos. Lucius always said that warriors should forever remember the origin of their own flesh and blood, just as lovers should always know the fundamental nature of their own hearts' desire. This seemed an odd thing for a Praetorian Guard to say, but Lucius often spoke of many strange things: in particular and in mesmerizing detail, he often spoke of his family and the line of his people all the way back to the beginning. The tenor of his voice never wavered, and the narrative remained oddly unchanged from one telling to the next. He explained how his family had descended from the mighty Kurgan tribes in the north, and how his bloodline had flowed like the rivers of my homeland until they met the sea, eventually intermingling with the Keltoi of the Nikaía area and then later with the Egyptians as his ancestors migrated throughout the decades of Greek conquest. Raised entirely in Alexandria, so he said, Lucius had followed in the long-standing traditions of his forefathers, joining the Roman Army as soon as he was of age: Warfare was in his blood. He claimed that it colored his every word and every gesture, but to me, it was all just the idle musings of a mercenary. I had heard it all before, many, many times, and yet, there was sincere affection behind the savagery.

The magnificence of his beloved Alexandria had not been lost on him, and the lands of his forefathers, which were mere visions in a dream, had left his soul lost with longing. The stories he recounted were so rich and so elaborate, so overly romanticized and beautiful, it was as if he had traversed those ancient lands himself. On occasion, his narration would move him to tears. Indeed, I was quite familiar with the callousness of soldiers, and this sentimentality seemed eerie and unnatural to me. How could a man with war imprinted upon his brow be so stricken with grief by the thought of anything less than Roman imperialism and ill-gotten gains? How could the barren and trampled soil of foreign lands—soil he could never have possibly felt beneath his feet—have thrust such compelling reminiscences upon him? It was utterly irrational and in complete opposition to all reason and common sense.

A life of hardship gives rise to skepticism, so I didn't believe his words. However subtly composed this poetry of his life appeared to be, I still felt the taint of intrigue upon his breath. Felt it so strongly that I couldn't help but exert the full force of my powers to delve deeper and expose the truths of his mind, but my efforts stank of futility. I gained nothing. Unable to penetrate the infinite blackness, I had no choice but to resign my trust unto him, even though his eyes betrayed a soul much older than his flesh would conceal.

As time went on, I began to fear my emotions less, and our attachment to each other grew: the need became obsessive; the trust—something real; the affection—more than a comfort. I became accustomed to his arbitrary fits of emotion, and he courteously respected my lack thereof. O the days we wasted away, lying idly by the fire, entangled in each other's arms—drinking wine, eating dried figs—and for a moment it seemed, languishing in dewdrops and desire, we could forget about the breeze.

We had so much to share, so much to give to one

another, yet time was against us always, so the exchange of knowledge between us became something of a frenetic quest. Burning away the long hours of the days and nights—our thoughts but whispers under the cover of starlight—we spoke of secrets: the secrets of time and space, of magic and eternal life, of fear, loathing, and all manner of dark beasts hidden in the obscurity, and as the sun rose before us at the dawn of each new day, we spoke of love…innocent and pure.

As the years melted away, our eyes rarely wandered from one another, and my refusal of other consort had spawned abundant hushed rumors—rumors of a forbidden love between a handsome Praetorian Guard and his exotic courtesan. It was all so utterly ridiculous, but when I was alone, in the grip of the night's sultry fevers, I could think of little else but Lucius. O how I suffered. Those endless tormented nights brought little sleep to my eyes and visited my heart with a crushing, relentless pain: How I ached for him, an ache that threatened the courage of my convictions and threatened my sanity.

Would it be love that caused such sublime misery and madness? Should I surrender to this love and allow its conquest? For if I did so, would I not then truly be a slave?

Many a long, restless hour I would brood over that question as the twilight passed into oblivion unnoticed, and it was on this very night, the blackest of nights, that the moon arose, full and luminous, in direct challenge to all of my petty arguments on the matter. Yes, the moon would indeed be my redeemer, and as I drew it down… its radiance issued forth, exploding gloriously within me like bolts of lightning through my veins. Then it all became clear. Yes! I would yield. I would yield to love and to Lucius—for it is, in truth, that a slave to love is not often so unlike a slave to hatred, and to suffer willingly as a slave to love seemed the lighter burden to bear.

I dressed hastily and ran from my quarters. It was time, time to give of myself for no other reason than I wanted to, but the corridor seemed endless, and my bare feet seemed to catch on every loose pebble as if they were shards of glass. When I finally edged the doorway, panting and trembling, I saw Lucius there waiting, ever solemn, ever patient, his still blue eyes fixed upon me as I caught my breath and walked unhurried into the room. However, calm as I might have appeared, my shadow— even after my conversation with the moon and all the justifications and self-righteous indignation—still clung to the thread of impending regret that had knotted itself around my neck so long ago. Alarmed by the intensity of Lucius' gaze, my shadow leapt up from the floor, and upon hitting the fire's sulfurous flames, it evaporated into a lingering grey mist...evaporated into nothingness.

And Lucius just smiled, as if the effect had resulted from his will alone. It was the smile of unadulterated confidence, and it nearly impaled me. I struggled again to breathe when he stood up and put a hand out to me, a hand worn, scarred, and strong. I could taste the regret in my mouth now as I watched the firelight flick across the flesh of his palm, as I watched it move over him to eventually alight upon his face, warming his skin and setting his eyes ablaze with white-hot embers as if they reflected the demon fires of *Hel*. In that moment, I felt a wall of heat slam into me, so I stepped backwards even as I felt the need to step forward. Didn't matter though, I stopped in mid-step when he asked me to.

"No, Selena…," he said as he walked towards me. "My only desire is to look upon you. The light suits you, and the amorous rouge from the fire favors you. Please —take off your robes."

I felt the earnestness in his voice as he closed the distance between us, and I felt the desire in his flesh, felt the urgency in his fingers when he brushed back the fall of hair that had been softly seducing my shoulders. He had been sitting by the fire for hours, and yet his hands were cold. I felt that cold against my neck, down my back, then again on my hips, and I shivered. In all the years we had shared company, Lucius had never once laid his hands upon me, so this request, this night, troubled me, but I felt compelled by my own desire, and so without hesitation, I did as I was told and surrendered the silken fabric to the floor.

My skin, pale, kissed gently by the heat of the fire, radiated its moonlit glow, and in the fitful incandescence, the sins of the blade wore heavily upon my flesh. Lucius circled around me, the palm of his hand here, the light touch of his fingertips there, and then he spoke my name as if demanding a confession. A confession to a question he had not yet asked, but I knew he would as I watched the last remnants of the smile he had held only moments before slip from his face. He took a step back, drew his sword, and then pointed it towards my scarred flesh.

"Men have made these?"

I couldn't recall ever feeling a sense of modesty let alone a sense of shame before, but the hurtful tone of his voice struck with precision, and all I wanted to do was cover myself. I knelt down and reached for my robes, but he abruptly moved in front of me and placed his foot upon them. "No, Selena, do not cover yourself. Sit down and answer my question."

Again, I did as he asked: I made my confession, made it through a flood of confused and unfamiliar emotions. I wanted to cry. I wanted to scream, but more importantly, for the first time, I actually wanted to *confess*. "Yes," I said, "men have made them: some of them, but not all. Many are of my own tormented will."

"And the others?"

He knew that I wasn't being entirely honest, that I had held back, so despite my discomfort, I proceeded to recount my time at the Vestal Temple and the futile trials to save my soul. He sheathed his sword and urged me to continue, but I didn't want to speak of my private battles. I didn't want to speak of the gruesome prophetic visions that had haunted me for as long as I had known what it was to be a woman. The rape of my body was easier to deal with than the rape of my mind, and I said as much even through his insistence that it mattered not. Firm of composure, without interjection, genuinely enthralled by every word, he sat next to me and listened. Listened to the pain. Listened to the shame. Listened to the lament of a soul who had since birth been destined for damnation, and upon my reaching the end of my deposition, he simply stared—through me—a vacant stare, without words or even the vaguest hint of emotion.

I had never really given much thought to what my body had endured over the years other than the fact that I had endured. I never invoked my scars for pity. To me, they were a testament to my fortitude, to my strength of will, and to my honor. Every time I looked at them, they reminded me who I was, what I was, and of the power I possessed. Each scar was a constant, faithful reminder of the torment and the misery that fate had gifted me, and more importantly, that I had survived it, had triumphed against it. However, Lucius' vacant stare set my teeth on edge. At his request, I had exposed myself beyond what I was accustomed to, and I expected something in return. That was how it worked, but I didn't know what I wanted from him. Affirmation? Reassurance? I didn't know, but I needed something. "No tears for my pain?" I asked in annoyance, since he shed them so willingly at all manner of other occasions, and maybe that is what had irritated me so. He had managed to get me to reveal my shame, the agony of my existence, and now I wanted payment …I wanted sympathy.

I wasn't going to get it.

Lucius stood up, took his sword and tossed it aside, and then slowly removed his tunic, laying bare an ethereal yet vigorous body. But his bronzed skin revealed an agony much more volatile than mine. It revealed the barren ages of time. The scars—many, deeper, more trenchant than my own—carved a purpose all their own into his flesh as they intertwined with the parallel lines of the winged serpent encircling his torso. The *man* had long ceased to be, and the warrior caged within bled through like so much spilled ink on tattered parchment.

"No tears for *your* pain?" he responded with the same level of bitterness I had used upon him. "I would sweet Selena, but you see…I have no tears for my own."

Arrogance abandoned, I misplaced my words and any shred of discretion that was left to me. Without hindrance or hesitation, I moved towards him, my fingers reaching out to him, longing for his flesh…

And he reached back.

He grasped my hand, pulled it to him, and pressed it earnestly to his chest. I felt the scars, felt their raised and ragged edges, and I felt the tremulous heaving of his breast and the rush of his pulse, feverish and well beyond his control. His body begged forgiveness, and I forgave him. Forgave him the sin of stealing my secrets from me. They were all I had of my own, but I had fallen in love with him, and forgiveness was no longer a choice. He could see it in my eyes, as I saw it reflected back from his into mine, and so he dug his hands into my hair, pulled me in, and kissed me, but only for a moment. A brief moment too swift and fleeting to take notice of. Faltering against my alleged maturities, he abruptly pulled away, ashamed, eyes cast to the floor almost as if he were awaiting a forthcoming criticism or admonishment.

I had none.

I couldn't understand his fear, so I put my hands upon his face and returned the gesture he had so inno-cently made with his kiss, and all I could taste was his want settling against mine. His lips, potent and persua-sive, tasted of honey—intoxicatingly sweet and yet utterly deceptive. I knew they cloaked a savage inner beast, but the embrace that seemed to have us locked together in spirit and will was a tender yet forceful surrender. His touch felt like velvet against my skin as his fingers ex-plored the wounds of my life, and all the awkwardness between us faded away as we descended in ecstasy to-wards the lowest depths of despair and desire we knew. For hours, we lay together, sometimes silent, sometimes not. When we did speak, we spoke of a great longing, and we shared in our agony through whispered affirmations and heated breath. We spoke of the future and of the past, and we spoke of the Cosmos as seen through our minds' eyes. He too had been possessed by the Logos, but his gift was much stronger than my own, more ancient and powerful: his visions—apocalyptic. I felt terrified and exhilarated. I felt a thousand black asps twisting and turning in my stomach, and I could feel the blood pounding in my veins. I yearned for his power, for his command of it.

I yearned to know the darkness of his soul.

And I would know it, as sure as I would know the darkness of my own, and we would begin with an ancient book: a book of secrets and shadow.

5

The Black Gates

T he iridescent scarab amulet that hung from Lucius' neck seemed to pulsate as he spoke, slowly, deliberately, in perfect time with the sacrosanct words. Swinging back and forth against his breath and against the gentle movements of his body, the weight of the gold reflected the restless light from the fire, and the sumptuous lilt of his voice and the alluring cadence of the words he spoke rose up above the crackling of the flames and the sound of my own blood rushing in my ears. "Hail, thou God Anniu," Lucius said, eyes shut tight as though fixing a prayer, and the walls of the room appeared to flex and ripple inward as the entreaty left off his breath in a whisper. "Hail, thou God

Pehrer, who dwellest in thy hall. Grant thou that my soul
may come unto me from wheresoever it may be, and if it
would tarry, then let my soul be brought unto me from
wheresoever it may be..." And the fire answered, reached
out to embrace his words, to lick them with soot and sin.
Its energy radiated through me, awakening urges I had
long ago suppressed in the grey places of my will. "Let
me have possession of my soul and of my spirit," the
prayer continued as if Lucius were begging it from *me*,
begging some sort of release and forgiveness I was unaware I was offering. I had never offered truth before.
Had never thought a man could want such a thing, but
he did. Lucius wanted the truth: "Let me be true of voice
with them wheresoever they may be..." He had said it.
Yes, he wanted the truth of his own soul. He spoke of
looking down upon his natural body, that it might rest
upon his spiritual body, and then he demanded that his
body neither perish nor suffer corruption forever, but
the words made so sense to me, no sense at all. He spoke
of death, and although I had longed for it often and had
pretended to understand my yearning for it, I had no
truth of it to give him. All I could think was that I
wanted to devour him—flesh, blood, and whatever remnants remained of his soul. His skin against mine and the
heat of his breath in my face had led me astray, led me
away from the words and into the depthless distance.

His initial thrust, insistent and deep, forged its way
through a lifetime of refusals I had so naively imagined
wanting to give myself over to. A feeling of lightness
consumed me then, and I realized I was feeling pleasure
for the first time: pleasure given freely, but to myself, so
long denied. I had been denied my own death, and in

that denial, I had been denied a life of my own making. My life had been bought and paid for with blood. Innocent blood. I could taste it, *his* blood, thick in my mouth, and the sweet elixir, his lips wet with it, threw my mind into a manic state of confusion. I wanted to sink my teeth into his flesh, my desire for him was that desperate. It was careless the way I...needed him.

"My love," he said, his want for me slipping into poetic repose as he placed the amulet around my neck. "My immortal beloved, you are my forever, Selena. I absolutely adore you, and everything that I am, and that I ever was, I give to you."

Everything. Had he offered me everything? I had never been offered anything of worth in my entire life, had never taken anything that wasn't already left to rot. Could this everything sate the ravenous hunger he had awakened within me? Could it? I didn't know what to do with my hands. I wanted to clasp them over my mouth to stop from shouting my devotion at him. The love I felt was dangerous, obscene, and my thoughts—chaotic—drifted through distance and time. I felt his heart racing beneath the palm of my hand. I felt his words reach out to me carried aloft by breath so sweet. *Everything.* I felt its dark hypnotic restraint pushing down on me. *I give to you.* I could not resist the seduction, could not resist my own need to *take* any longer, and so I surrendered myself completely: to his words, to his lips, to the lascivious rhythm of his hips. Each thrust, fuelled by love, slick with an unbounded rage—grinding away all the years of emptiness—was matched in strength only by my own unbearable desire, and as we tore at each other's flesh, I looked upon my lover's face, or rather, looked upon what I had so stupidly accepted as my salvation. I should have told him I loved him, but in that moment, all I felt was a dread chill slip over me when I came to understand that the *everything* came with a price. When I looked up into Lucius' eyes, once so fierce and so full of light, I saw nothing but a crimson distance. There was a need in the darkness there I had not noticed before, a covetousness of vile proportions. His eyes, now cored with fire and hatred, bore into me, and the amulet, blistering hot, settled itself against my skin, searing my breast almost to the bone.

As the pain scraped away at my sanity, I no longer felt consumed by the tender embrace of a lover: I felt nothing of love. Lucius' passionate assault, now agonizing, left me raw with anguish. The *everything* I had so wanted had turned to nothing. Worse than nothing. I had sought a soul that might endure mine, but I would not find it here. What could I ever possibly be to him? A wife? A lover? Someone to conceive an eternity with? I was a whore. I could never feel what he needed me to feel. I felt only the carnage unleashed by a starving animal. I felt shame. I felt regret, each inflicting burning wounds upon my will. *I shall owe my life and all my happiness to him.* The price to be paid was nothing more than another servitude, and in that knowledge—my soul rent with heartbreak—I let loose a wavering cry for mercy. I begged him to stop, thrust my fists against his chest, but my pleas fell to little purpose.

"It is but the quickening," he said, justifying the violence through clenched teeth as he held me down, firmly and securely. "Just be still, my love. Do not resist it, Selena. It is best. The pain is less if you do not resist it." But the pain he spoke of was beyond my physical body. My body felt nothing. Having no might left to resist, it had wilted at the torment, but more importantly, my heart had gone cold, stopped beating entirely, and I wept. I wept a flood of agony as the black gates opened …as ghastly and horrifying images bit into my eyes.

At last, I was *offered* what I had desired for so many years: I would finally be allowed my trespass. At last, I could see all the truths of his mind. *He* had allowed it, at last, and when I finally stopped screaming, I was lost in the darkness, standing alone in the scorched sand amid the great pyramids. There, in a sliver of twilight breaching time itself, they eclipsed the sun, and the moon, full and ripe with blood, hung low and bloated in the sky. Pyres blazed in front of me and behind me. The flames rose almost to the heavens, charring the edges of infinity and illuminating the twilight with streaks of emptiness while off in the distance, ancient priests, cloaked as otherworldly creatures, recited spells and invocations into the night air. I felt the force of their words, though I could not understand them. I felt the power in them, felt a spell tugging at me from beyond what I knew of this world, and I felt fear—real fear. My body shook to its core, and every inch of my flesh was covered in a film of cold, stale sweat.

In an attempt to calm my shattered and violated mind, Lucius held my face in his hands and breathed a stream of soothing endearments into my mouth. The sweetness of tone mixed with my own desperate gasps for mercy settled over me in a fugue of futility, and so I acquiesced to the undeniable suggestions of his will—deliberate and rhythmic now—as he reached out to me in tenderness, but it was a bittered tenderness, offering little succor or satisfaction. My wounds were too deep for a casual caress, the ache too formidable. I was just too weak, too pathetic and weak. My need was too great …and the pain…the pain diminished the moment I cast aside any thought of salvation, but the endearments he lavished upon me, as smooth and calculated as they were, could not hinder the gloom as it moved, shadowing my consciousness with regret unimaginable. Its fluidic murk surrounded everything, dimming the fire as it sought to soften the moment's sharp edges.

"I am sorry, Selena," he said, his hands in my hair.

"I love you," he said again…and then in the distance again. "I never meant to hurt you," he confessed as he covered my mouth with his hand and thrust himself further into the darkness. "Forgive me, please," he asked, once I had stopped weeping, but his words fell as hollow as his apology upon my ears, and the comforts he proffered faded under the weight of the anguish he had put upon me. His lovelorn declarations seemed too trivial and insincere to allay my contempt, and like regurgitated bile from the depths of oblivion, my hatred erupted—erupted at the height of our union—and as his body trembled, wracked with vile pleasure, I, with the frenzy of a madman, clawed the flesh from his throat, threw him from my body to the floor, and then stood mighty over his struggle.

"Forgiveness…," I said after I took a deep breath. "Alas, Lucius, I am not as frail as the flower petals you violated me upon. I have no faith in forgiveness, and you have no right to ask it of me. I will bear my injury, and *forgiveness* will come from your maker, *my Lord*."

In that moment, my nude body stained with the sin of his soul, I transcended all uncertainty. I had never asked for his love. He had seduced me, had forced my descent. I had never wanted love, and as his life ebbed away in the viscous crimson mire collecting beneath my feet, I came to the realization that I had, in fact, needed it.

This was a bitter draught to swallow, and no amount of weeping would help wash it down. I cast aside all hope, as there would be none.

None for me.

None for the world.

I am the Hidden One in the hidden place.
I am a perfect spirit among the companions of Râ,
And I have gone in and come forth
Among the perfect souls.

I am the shadow of Nehebkau.
I am the mighty Soul of saffron-colored form.
I have come forth from the underworld at pleasure.
I have come.
I have come forth from the Eye of Horus.
I have come forth from the underworld with Râ
From the House of the Great Aged One in Heliopolis.
I am one of the spirits who would come forth from the
Underworld.
Grant thou unto me the things in which my body needeth,
A heaven for my body,
A hidden place for my soul.

May the God, who himself is hidden,
Whose face is concealed,
Who shineth upon the world in his forms of existence,
And in the underworld,
Grant that my soul may live forever!
Grant thou unto me an entrance and an exit
Without let or hindrance.

6

Divine Providence

T hose words resounded in my ears like the
heavy rolling claps of thunder willed upon
the shoreline by an angry sea, and they
pounded out a purpose even the Gods couldn't fathom. I
had no idea where those words came from, but they fell
from my lips as if I had always known them. I chanted
them again and then again as I stared down at Lucius'
pallid body.

What had I done?

Flower petals clinging to his face, his body lay
stained with self-sacrifice. O my lovely Lucius, the only
thing chaste in my life, and I had destroyed it. I could
take the blame for what I had done even though it had

been done under coercion. It was this place. This vile place had consumed me. Its avarice and decadence flowed freely, poisoning the hearts of its people. I had been poisoned, poisoned by the hands that had claimed to be my salvation, hands that had beaten, ravaged, and violated my body, and then in an instant offered absolution. But alas, a few coins over my eyes would not wash away the sin from my soul.

I took up Lucius' sword, and the weight of it in my hand startled me. It had no weight at all, and the slightness of burden shot a sense of liberation through me—cold, calculated, and cruel—as if it had some miraculous and divine power to release me from my bonds. This power rose up, swelled in my veins. Its ugliness invaded me: I hated myself. I hated the world, and the amulet around my neck seemed to pulsate with affirmation.

Yes, hatred. It moved through my rotting flesh, surrounded my aching heart. Indeed, hatred was the price, and for redemption, I was more than willing to pay. I had killed the only man I had ever loved. I had lost my soul, so what was there left to lose by accepting hatred as my savior.

I sliced through the air several times, allowing my body to adjust to the blade's tone and texture. It shimmered as it caught its own reflection in the firelight, and I knew then that divine providence lay just beyond its sharpened tip. There was no catharsis in this knowledge, for even though my liberation was at hand, I was merely an open wound, filthy and desiccated: only what once had been a wound embracing the sword was now a wound wielding it. But I had no time to relish my new-found liberation. I had taken a life. Rome would rise up against me now. I had to make my escape; there was no other choice, no other path for me to take.

I stole from the room whatever gems and coin I could carry and then dressed myself in Lucius' uniform. I tied my hair up and crept out into the torch-lit hallway, but my stealth was not only absurd, it was self-defeating. It wouldn't have mattered if I were to have ridden a chariot through the place: no one could possibly have heard me over the debauched animal thrusting and slick groans of deviant satisfaction.

I felt the rancid burn of bile surge up in my throat, so I swallowed hard, slipped into the darkness, and made my way to the stables in search of a horse. Upon entering, my eyes began to water. The stench was unbearable, and most of the horses were overcome with sweat and restlessness, having been beaten and worked to exhaustion before arriving. But there was one: one magnificent beast that tamed the hatred in my heart long enough for me to feel the aching in my soul again. A mighty steed he was, imposing not only in physique but in demeanor as well —regal, proud, and black as the center of midnight. I stepped into the stall. There was no fear in his eyes. He leant into me, shifting his snout underneath my arm— not in submission, but in amity—as if he somehow knew that I belonged to him as much as he belonged to me. Our hope, our purpose, might have been tarnished by our own wretched existences, but it was the same. I cradled his head in my arm and slid my other hand down his neck, under his braided mane, and then across his chest to his leg. A tremor rippled through the muscles at the command of my touch, and I looked deeply into his eyes—forlorn, broken, but not spiritless—and the amulet glittered as it reflected back within. Yes, he bore his hatred with pride, just as I bore mine with indifference, and so it was agreed.

Despite the fact that I hadn't ridden since I was a child in Germania, I didn't seem to be afflicted with a sense of awkwardness or trepidation in the slightest. I threw a blanket over the animal's back, and once I leapt atop, I felt exalted.

Dominions would fall under hoof and blade, would fall beneath and before me—the Universe's appointed executioner—and I would drink their blood stained pleas for mercy as if it were the water of life. My lips would be forever parched, my thirst forever insatiable.

Invoking the Gods of fire and blazing with an immeasurable hatred, I rode out to the very portico of the brothel and reduced the entire building and all its occupants to cinders. Everything I touched, everything I saw or possessed even a passing thought of burst into flames, and while watching that vile memory disintegrate into dust, I was overcome with joy, a joyous satisfaction. Nevertheless, it served no purpose other than to whet my thirst for blood and further harden my heart. I sheathed my sword and turned my back on Rome. I turned my back forever, leaving the sad pathetic excuse for a life I had once known in a cloud of fire and brimstone. Trampling the earth, I fled its abuses, incinerating all in my path.

I fled to the very edge of the known Universe. To the land of mighty warriors...I fled to Sarmatia.

KEEPING TO THE SHADOWS, I rode every day from the illusory veil of dusk until the faint-hued incandescence of dawn. I rode over barren mountainous regions cloaked in bitter cold and ice. I rode down through lush dew-laden valleys, and I rode over the rock-strewn shores of great inland seas. My journey took many moons as I moved through the Roman Empire. I felt neither hunger nor thirst nor cold, and even without sustenance or sleep, my body grew hardened, powerful, unaffected by the ravages of time and elemental trespass. My spirit had been re-forged, twisted and cast anew from the destructive force that had overtaken me. My soul and body could no longer be conquered, defeated, or subdued. Fear had oft been my betrayer, its ever-present restraint felt against my will like a beast gnawing in contentment at a decaying carcass. But that beast had slunk away in the night, and the carcass was now set ablaze. Its smoldering flesh would forever light my way in the darkness.

Eventually, the end of my journey drew near as the starlit obsidian sky opened up around me. I had reached my destination: a sprawling windswept stretch of fertile lands. Far reaching, its splendorous landscape, much to my surprise, exceeded the beauty and virtue of my own estranged homeland. As I moved across the steppe, the boundless pastoral grasslands and the nomadic tribal life induced a sense of freedom in me that I had not experienced since childhood, and for the first time in my adult life, I actually felt the wind in my hair. With each stray settlement I passed, I imagined that I could be happy there and could live there. I imagined the dawn shimmering violets over the rippling sways of grass. I imagined a peasant life, a simple life.

In time, I discovered that I had a seraphic agility for moving about unnoticed, a wraith shifting among the legions. I passed through many encampments and small settlements, and it was as if the people saw a kinship in me. They saw past the Roman uniform—saw past my physical presence entirely as if I did not exist in body at all. I knew their languages as if I had spoken them since birth. I knew everything: their histories, their struggles, and their victories. They broke bread with me and shared libation, shelter, conversation, and comforts. I was grateful beyond measure and vowed to repay the kindness, even if it meant sacrificing myself. I was willing to die, but the Gods would not ask as much of me. Not yet. For the lives I would be tasked to take, regrettably, did not include my own. The will of the Gods would not allow it, and more importantly, my will would not allow it, for I breathed not air but vengeance.

I would spend many an age in Sarmatia, learning the ways of war. I took tremendous comfort in the strength of its people as they battled endlessly to preserve their way of life against all adversity. They became my teachers, my brethren, and my muse. The mounted archers of the steppe: children of the Amazonians…and ferocious warriors in their own right. Their women were proud, strong-armed huntresses and fighters. My presence was welcomed, and my place—assured.

Still, as inevitable as the sun's rising, Rome would infect these lands, their treachery crawling over it like a festering plague, and blood was shed almost daily.

Fortunately, Æolic stealth and the sheer magnitude of my hatred contributed significantly to the battlefield. There was no greater joy to be found in life than that of taking up arms with your brethren. Not to mention, the act of slaughtering Roman soldiers was most satisfying. I never washed the blood from my hands, and yet, despite all my rage, victory would be elusive, for Marcus Aurelius, in a series of bloody and protracted battles, would eventually pacify the region. In defeat, wounds stinging, I left my beloved warriors then and moved onward to Germania: my long forgotten home.

TRAVELLING THE LENGTH of the great river Danube, from Black Sea to Black Forest, I passed more peoples than I had ever encountered in Sarmatia: bold and defiant clans, humble nomadic herders, and the rulers of great kingdoms. The river offered itself to these people over kilometers of varied landscapes, and I clung to its shores as a lifeline until I left its embrace as I made my way towards the Rhenus.

"The rivers and the sea will lead you home..." My father had always said that to me as I drifted off to sleep at night. It had been so long since I heard his voice in my dreams, but I would always remember those words.

The Rhenus: the river of life. Its crystalline water rises from the precipitous altitudes of the Raetian Alps, and I followed it as it veered slightly westward, nourishing the land with liquid flows of ice and snow while carving its path through rock and stone as it flowed steadily towards the Germanic Sea...and my homeland amid the mist and shadow. Great Gods had forged this land. Taking hammer to steel, they had released their wrath on the sea, unleashing its fury upon the rocky shoreline. Untamed, it swells and surges around broad peninsulas and vast islands, girdling the northern parts of the country and fringing the coasts with majestic cavernous fjords. No man could know an Eden unless he has stood and heard his own heart echoed back to him from the densely forested rock of the fjords.

Yes, all this breathtaking beauty, so affecting, yet wasted by war for centuries, with much blood shed among its own peoples. The dust of my ancestors lay just beneath the surface of the soil, their shadows crested with the waves, and their voices echoed sweetly upon gentle breezes through the wood. One thousand moons. My history was nothing more than a tempest of allusion, my home was no longer my home, and the remembrances of my youth now escaped me. Nevertheless, I remained with those of my own descent, for I was bound to them out of a mutual hatred for the Romans. I would witness many brutal sieges as the machine of war —unstoppable—laid lands to waste in its wake, the fertile soil soaked through with the stagnant blood of its peoples. Even so, the Germanic tribes were strong, stronger than Rome. Their steadfast determination was the indestructible iron foundation of their spirit. Time was all that they required…that and the stout sword of retribution: my sword.

Germania persevered, I persevered, and by the forces of might or madness, the clans pushed across the limes of the Danube, spurring civil wars all the way to the Rhenus. The battle cries echoed and then, mixed with blood and mist, died away upon the wind as foot soldiers and legions of cavalry shook the earth. The hammering pulse of war, it shook the earth all the way to Gallia, the beloved lands of Lucius' forefathers, the land of the Celts and their mystical Druid priests.

To the Romans, it had been so named Gaul.

The territories inhabited by the ancient Celts had

long ago fallen to the Roman scourge. Their tribes were weakened. Lacking order, substance, and any shred of true leadership, they were scattered, pit against one another for survival. Through Emperor Claudius, the Druids were forcibly subdued and their native deities were replaced with Roman counterfeits. But the Celtic peoples persisted. In secrecy, they made their revolt, and ultimately, Gaul would be lost to the Roman Empire forever by means of repeated Germanic invasions— invasions that would, in the end, lead me to the lush, emerald green isles of Britannia, and utterly captivated by the mysteries of the land and its peoples, I decided that I would remain.

7

Mongrels, Cannibals, *and Human Sacrifice*

The Celts: the barbarian hordes, or so legend tells us. One might envision a rabid and mangy pack of wild dogs, but as I rode through the spring flush of rain into their midst, I came to see that legends can be inaccurate. In this case, heinously inaccurate, for the Celts weren't the tattooed cannibalistic savages the Roman's had decreed them to be. And while the glen I had entered, with its stone monoliths eclipsing the sun, might have been Pan's labyrinth, demon faeries of the wood the Celts were not. I would know. To consort with the shadows does not a monster make. I was the monster who'd walked into their world, a world of beautiful people who lived and worshiped according to the laws of a social order well ahead of their time.

It was as if I had ridden into a myth. Elected Kings led the tribes, and the society as a whole was divided using a rudimentary cast system. The warriors, deemed the noble upper class, rose above all else in rights and privileges. Then there were the intellectuals, or rather, the revered ones, which included the Druids, the poets, and the scholars, and lastly there came the commoners: the merchants, traders, farmers, herders, and pretty much everyone else. As it was so with the Sarmations and with my own Germanic heritage, freeborn women, seldom looked upon as lesser beings, participated as equals in warfare and kingship. Their honor and skill in battle were widely acknowledged and prized above all else by the men of the tribes.

To be a learned warrior woman was something of an anomaly though, and I—with my uncanny knowledge of antiquity and my battle scarred body—was looked upon as a Goddess, at the very least a bearer of good fortune and victory in battle. Their name for my kind was the *Morrigan*, but I had many names in many lands.

As far as the barbaric cannibal horde designation, I didn't find this to be truth. It was all nothing more than Roman propaganda, and I found them to be no more savage than any other culture I had encountered. While I would agree that Celtic society lived for combat, it was more sport fighting—camaraderie for survival, if you will—focusing on good-natured raids and hunting expeditions rather than territorial conquests. Sadly, this was their greatest failing. The idea of killing off another culture for profit and dominance was an idea that required strategy and ruthless cunning. In that way, the

Celts were too primitive, their Gods too ineffectual. The more organized Romans and Germanic tribes effectively pulled their lands right out from under their own feet.

I felt their plight, its acid ate away at my bones for I knew what it was like to have your life taken away, to have your heritage obliterated, but what would extend my stay with the Celts was not their plight, their strength, or their ferocity, nor was it their cultural elegance or my own anger. It was something less tangible that roused my desire: it was their mysticism and religious beliefs, which arrested my soul and mirrored my own long-standing belief in the Logos.

Celtic deities were wide-ranging, multitudinous, and varied greatly from tribe to tribe. Such a lush tapestry cluttered the culture with appreciable religious differences, although worship was fairly consistent across the lands. Borne of the earth and forever to be cast back into the earth, prayer and ceremony—no matter the God or tribal idiosyncrasy—were conducted always in sacred groves—stone temples of varying size and shape, maintaining blessed trees and votive pools—at which I would sequester myself for countless hours, indulging my need for the Logos with magic, myth, legend, and other mystical bewitchments that could only be whispered in the dark. Or so taught the Druid scholars.

Taking respite from the battlefield was a comfort so rare that I made the most of every opportunity available to me, and the Druids had knowledge and insights into many things, including the workings of the Cosmos.

But a Druid is not always a High Priest. This is a common misconception. The image of the bearded necromancer of the wood—flowing white robes—chalice and staff in hand—always comes to mind. Laughable, but it does. We can blame modern fiction for that because that image couldn't be more inaccurate, for a Druid, by Celtic definition, was any well-educated member of the society. Although, the most educated were often priests and heralds, as these intellectual pursuits required very particular talents and aptitudes for their practices. Those very talents and aptitudes were most intriguing to me. So given my own peculiar abilities, my need for knowledge waxed favorably, and I spent much of my time with the priests—the exalted *High Priests*—who compiled the magical transcriptions, divined the tribe's vigor in future years, and attended to the religious festivals, including the ritual sacrifices of crops, animals…and humans.

Sacrifice was not unknown or offensive to me, for I had witnessed ritualistic slaughter in some form or another since childhood. One might even say that war is a form of ritualistic slaughter in a sense, and far less barbaric than some of what the Romans called *games.*

Milky shadows oft pass over the religious practices of ancient cultures, and I would be negligent if I held my own tongue in these matters. Human sacrifices were quite uncommon. Even in my own homeland, the practice was infrequent. But the fact of the matter is: human sacrifice was and is part of human culture. Celtic society was no exception, and most of the human sacrifices were restricted to the execution of convicted criminals. I witnessed no human sacrifice outside of very specific and regulated festivals.

The cheering, the chanting, the taste of salt in the air as droplets of blood sprayed the slabbering mass of people, stinging their eyes as they tried to look past the sun's glare into the soul of the damned. Yes, festivals they were, for the Celts had a sublime diversity to their savagery. To say that I didn't admire or find it exhilarating would be deceit beyond measure. One cannot refute or discount humanity's dark heart. Those executions, if viewed today, might be considered performance art, and as much as they were offensive, they were also morbidly exquisite. Among the most barbaric and the most striking that I witnessed were those sacrifices practiced in the course of Essus worship. Essus was, give or take tribal semantics, the benevolent God of Justice. However, in the case of societal waste, merciless torture was not only permitted but also savored as a decadent and gratifying leisure activity.

Bound and gagged with goat intestines, the offenders would be dragged to their doom: mud caked to twisted and bared feet, flies and other vermin caught against parched lips and dried teeth. Kicking. Screaming. Fists clenching their hair, they would be led to a great temple in which a mighty oak tree had erupted through an aperture in the roof. They would then be taunted by the crowd, rocks flying from every direction as the priests chanted over their bodies, which were stripped bare and then hung from the oak's branches until dead. On occasion, they would be set ablaze until charred, and at other times, their stomachs would be sliced open, allowing my kindred, the carrion crows, to pluck out their eyes and feast upon their slick dripping entrails.

Invaders, whether they were a rival tribe or foreign force, met with similar savagery, as the Celts also severed the heads from their deceased adversaries.

Headhunters, cannibals, call them what you will, as a matter of faith, they believed the spirit, or the essence of the warrior, resided within the head. Taking a head in battle was the utmost subjugation of an opponent, and such were the laws of chaos. By divine right, a head not only bestowed prestige upon the triumphant warrior, but it also endowed the warrior and his family with a slave for eternity. A commodity very much in high demand. This head collecting was such a venerated ritual that the heads were often displayed proudly as trophies, impaled on pikes and left to rot in the sun like bloated maggot-infested meat-puppets: a gruesome reminder that death is always victorious.

I could appreciate that, but I required neither trophy nor slave in the afterlife. I, duty bound, had no ego or sense of justice to placate. I, purely out of malice and hatred, collected countless heads in the coming eons of darkness as I watched Rome retreat and fall just as I had foretold it while under the spell of the Vestal Flame. Germanic invasion intensified. There was nothing I could do to stop it, and by the mediaeval period, much of the cultural heritage of the Celtic peoples had been transformed. Their might and their magic had forever disappeared into the mists of time, and their legacy fell to ruin, reduced to common folk superstition and fable, much like my own existence.

The years seemed endless. There was no afterlife for me, no rest, no divine transcendence, no dreams of eternal peace, nothing. Stumbling backwards and forwards, time had lost all significance or purpose. It taunted me with its irony, and I had only the power to remain still

and watch and wait…wait for the change in seasons…
wait for the stars to burn out in the sky.

I watched the wrack and ruin of Rome's once indom-
itable fortresses. I witnessed the birth of black-winged
dragons and dark sorcery. I fell humbled at the rise of
chivalry and romantic love, so much so that I cheered
the just and rightly earned ruination of abject demented
kings and jeered the heartfelt follies of courageous
knights. A scavenger of souls, I stood unmoved amid the
holocaustic aftermaths of idolatry, bloody religious cru-
sades, and the creeping doom of one thousand and one
plagues.

Yes, I watched in disbelief and astonishment as the
primitive world of my origin made way for the ages of
reason. Pseudo-civilized societies, ruled by religious and
feudal dogmas, erected magnificent cities in praise of
burgeoning new economies and Gods, monuments in
themselves to a truly modern age. And I remained…
largely in part because of the people: great writers, paint-
ers, architects, and philosophers sprang up all around
me, rivaling those of my youth. And I waited…as man's
depravity, suffused with heat and viciousness, reigned
victorious over the world.

I remained in London for no other reason than because I fell in love with a bridge—a bridge crowded with
gothic buildings up to seven stories in height, with
houses, shops, and even an intricately adorned chapel,
soaring directly to the heavens at its center.

The rivers and the sea will always lead you home.

That mediaeval bridge, spanning the Thames, had
nineteen small arches and a massive drawbridge of wood
and iron. Rock-clad gatehouses stood, ominous and fore-

boding, flanking each end like macabre sentinels. The southern, *The Stone Gateway*, would become a monument to human brutality and would forever be recorded by historians as one of London's most notoriously wicked sights.

On approach to the gate, one would be accosted by a grisly retrospective: mauled, mangled, and desiccated heads—purportedly traitors—that had been immersed in hot tar in order to preserve them against the elements and then subsequently impaled upon charred wooden pikes.

Hair matted and ragged, eyes burned from the sockets, mouths sewn closed to stop them screaming in the shadows, their contorted faces stood as a warning, a beacon to suffering and a testimony to man's barbarity. There they stood, alone in the darkness, soulless, pitiless, for all to see far and wide, and I stood with them, sword and grim purpose at hand.

The rivers and the sea had led me here, and I was home…

Forever.

8

Pale Horse ... *Pale Rider*

For a thousand years I remained, battle-worn and bloodied, as the tyranny of man consumed the whole of humanity. For another thousand, I waited, enrobed in the stealthy cover of twilight: stalking—a mythical phantom—silent and ever-patient—haunting the dimly-lit stairwells and the shaded corners of the world...my lips stained red with such foul whispered words. The truth, by its very nature, can be merciless, and so could I. If I spoke a truth to you, then it was time...and there would be no escaping your fate.

The city stank of regret, economic casualties, and shattered dreams. Welcome to the modern age where apathy and convenience are the new plagues, and the filthy rats spreading the diseases just have better tailors. It didn't take me long to find Nigel, once a spirited student of medicine. He was only thirty years old when heroin took its grim and deathly hold, his life reduced to nothing more than the needle's bloody backwash. Sure, he was intelligent and probably handsome at one point, intelligent enough to graduate from university without really even trying and handsome enough to bed any woman he wanted—again, without really even trying— so it seemed unlikely that he could be seduced by a false prophet, but he had, because he was not strong willed enough to resist the temptation and inner peace that only death can bring. He would give up everything to worship an illusion. So potent was its euphoric lure that his existence, in the end, would revolve around it. He had to have it, and with each fix, he got a little bit closer to the edge. Trading sex for death was just a vile means to that end. He had already sold his soul, and what was left of his body had outlasted its usefulness, now nothing more than an ill-fitting skin suit woefully out of fashion.

One day you wake up in the morning and just can't remember a time when you were happy, can't remember your past or the future you had once dreamt of. Can't remember who the face in mirror belongs to, and that's when you realize that life is not as beautiful and full of promise as you were once told that it was. Nigel just stared back at me with black, empty eyes. The hollow had taken away his beauty. Would that I could have seen it. For me, there was never beauty in the world: no life, no love, no beauty—only despair and decay. Death was always there, lying in wait in the midst of the fog and the storm clouds, slinking about in the noonday's shadows.

Just beneath the surface of everything, there it was: an endless rotting. You can smell it on their breath, the ones who have succumbed to it *and* the ones who haven't yet but will, and on one of the countless, dismally never-ending evenings on which I felt the dread compulsion to walk the streets of London with my nose to the air, I came upon him—rain-soaked, ragged—strung-out on the street corner. The world is filled with caricatures, archetypes, martyrs, saviors, and fiends, and Nigel had no idea which one to be anymore.

"Want to go for a *ride*?" I offered, and he accepted, but then again, I rarely got a refusal. When you beckon death to come calling, you always do so ready to accept what is offered. I suppose that is part of the rotting, the delusional acceptance of one's fate.

Not much later, the evening ebbed away in silence as we lay on the floor of his dingy flat. Even the cockroaches, scuttling across the rotted floorboards here and there through trails of dried vomit and rat excrement, had the good sense to ignore us. Consumed by ravenous appetites, we had fallen upon each other: victims of our own need, minds and naked limbs a tangled mass of discontent and disillusionment amid the strewn debris of his life. A tap dripped in the flat down the hall, someone was weeping quietly to themselves in the alley just outside the window, and the bats in the attic stretched their leathery wings...and waited. Nigel was already ridiculously high when I suggested we cook up another hit, but it was what he wanted. I always know what they want, even before they do.

"It will make the sex so much better," I explained with a grin, knowing all the while that I had lied to him;

although the subterfuge was unnecessary, as he would have complied regardless. Once a soul has surrendered to the urgings of their shadow, it takes a rare miracle indeed to bring them back. I was no such miracle. Yes, I answered their prayers—with deceit. That's no secret, so he nodded, and I smiled at him again and then picked up the butane torch.

Ritual. Living is a ritual, and so is dying.

It's as much about the process as it is the release. The surreal blue flicker of the butane and the acrid stench of the filthy boiling liquid lent a tomblike quality to the flat. The vapors, filled with a hatred so potent no witch would have the courage to conjure it on her own, hurled us into an obscure, dark, and intimate place. A place only the dead would dare go for solace.

I slid the syringe between my teeth, climbed atop him, and took him in. He shuddered reflexively at the force and heat of my thrust, and then he smiled and held his ravaged arm out to me as if his sagging skin were only a minor inconvenience. There was little life left in him as it was. The veins had collapsed ages ago, leaving behind long thick scars and open puss-filled wounds. His body was slowly dissolving into the murk, as was his erection inside of me. Shame really. To have one's mind riddled with maggots is one thing, but to have your manhood stripped from you, well, that is quite another. He shifted his hips upward in a feeble attempt to make amends, to satisfy me on some small level, but my desire had waned as well. He mouthed an apology, and I told him not to worry: "Your shame is too old for you," I said, and then I touched his face and looked upon him one last time. The half-lidded eyes that had, at first, appeared to me so vacant revealed a gentle soul, a soul long buried that had lost all hope of release. There was no shame in that, and he knew it. He strained a weak smile at me, all cheekbones jutting through thin grey skin, but I had given him his truth. There was nothing more to be said. No more effort needed, so I drove the needle into his arm as deeply as I drove my tongue into his mouth. He thrust upwards into me once, twice, and then his body fell silent. My spit was still wet on his lips, and the scent of my sex still lingered upon his flesh when he passed quietly into the haze.

The memory of him would have remained with me a bit longer if I hadn't found Elise almost by accident the very next night.

Elise, the young sweet thing. "The apple of my eye," her mother would say to her while foisting a condescending opinion at her down the length of a rigid bony finger, and Elise would ingratiate herself, if only for the moment. Rebellion just felt natural, like a prerequisite to adulthood, so being labeled a little wild child of the X-generation didn't seem such a cliché after all. She could tolerate the finger pointing: there were no real consequences, so what did it matter?

To the outside world, even those closest to her, she was cheerful, well adjusted, and exuded a genuine love of life. "A shiny new penny" people often said of her. However, underneath that vivacious and affable exterior —the bouncy red hair, the apricot sheen of her lips, and the quiet blue of her eyes—the twenty–one year old grappled with a hopelessness utterly beyond her control. She was not of a strong mind. She was, in fact, incredibly weak when it came to the opinions of others, more impor-

tantly, their opinions and perceptions of *her*. Could she
ever be perfect enough? Popular enough? Smart enough?
Pretty enough? As if any of it mattered. But it did. What
she adamantly claimed didn't matter was actually everything she needed. There is something to be said for one's
own perception, how it can be so easily manipulated and
distorted, but I was tired of walking and tired of pondering the existential conundrums of the dysfunctional. I
just wanted a drink.

The bar was rank with the intermingled stench of
sweat and liquor, as the seedier establishments always
are. It had an Americanized *dive* feel to the place, dark
and dirty, and the music box thrummed with the latest
annoying pop song of the day. Elise was hard *not* to notice, and so I sat there sipping my whiskey slowly as I
watched her undulating, oozing sex onto the dance floor
—inhibitions thrown to the wind. To look at her, she
didn't appear all that different from other party-girls of
her age. The bar was packed with them: flirting, gig-
gling, twirling their hair and batting their eyelashes, all
the while trying to act mature and seductive, blissfully
unaware of their inner feminism and just how dangerous
it was to be flinging it about so carelessly like their lit
cigarette ashes. I knew how dangerous it was. I waived
for the barmaid to bring me another drink, or rather, the
bottle. She smiled a tired slovenly old smile, nodded
towards me, blew a sweat-soaked ringlet of hair from her
forehead, and then headed off to the bar to fetch my
drink. As my eyes moved over the room, their intended
destination indeterminate, that's when I noticed that *He*
was watching Elise as well, his skin clammy and sour
with anticipation, his upper lip trembling almost imper-

ceptibly as he ran his tongue over the lower. His sweat smelled of hot gun-metal in the rain; it smelled of hunger.

I closed my eyes and breathed it in as a blast of heat hit me in the face. I felt flames in my hair, tasted smoke in the back of my throat, and my thoughts turned to the future as my fingers went numb and the terrible violations that he had planned for her suddenly burned into my eyes. Yes, he would use his cunning charms to lure her so innocently into the cellar of his home. He was too handsome: his smile too white, his tie too expensive, and his manner too perfect. "Your skin is soft like a rose petal," he would say as he kissed the words into the nape of her neck, and she would blush with conceit. He had nice things: art, fine furniture, good wine. He would offer her a drink, and she wouldn't see it coming, the blow to the head too quick, too sharp. She would slip to the floor, and he would sink to his knees praising his salvation: that white white smile now too wide, too sadistic. He might admire her for a while, a little snip at her clothes here and there with a pair of sharp scissors, but she wouldn't wake. Couldn't wake, and it wouldn't matter. Warm, cold, he didn't care. The post would hold her up. The splintered, nail-riddled wooden post in the center of the room. A structural support, he called it. The post would hold her up, the rope would hold her still while he touched all the soft places, touched them and then cut them. He would cut her slowly, taking his time to savor each stroke, to marvel at each piece of flesh that fell from her bones, and then when he had had enough playing with her blood, when it had gone cold and began to dry on his skin, he would shoot her twice in the face before cooking and eating her. Bits of seared flesh stuck between his teeth as he smiled that wide, white smile.

I thought I would vomit, and then I did. I doubled over in my seat while my stomach promptly returned the whiskey I had just drunk to the table. I could taste blood in it.

I wanted to kill him myself, but that was not for my kind. He did not beg for death, and so I could not answer. His desire was beyond my sphere of influence. His punishment was not mine to give. He would be winged to his rest soon enough though. I could at least take comfort in that. He turned and looked straight at me as if I had stripped the veneer from his soul. I poured myself another shot from the bottle that had been deposited at my table, and then I raised the glass in the air towards him and smiled. "Until then," I said to myself, "May the demons whisper nursery rhymes *to you*, good sir." He looked at the floor, looked around the room, a cursory glance here and a nervous nippy one there. He looked confused, and then he looked back to me, and I just continued to smile at him. His discomfort was amusing, but it was of no consequence. I did have my duty to uphold. He would not get to indulge his depraved urges…not that night. He wanted a clean one, but he would have to settle for a moll instead because I slit Elise's throat myself—quick and painless.

The how never seemed to matter as much as the why. The venue mattered even less than that. For me, every urine soaked rat's nest, every distressed doorway silhouetted in the gloom, and every crimson-stained cobblestone looked the same to me, but I can remember the moon on that night. I remember how it mocked the shadows and set the rain-battered pavement of the alley to a starlit shimmer, how it appeared to be in awe at the cold calculated mastery with which I performed my grim endeavor. How, for a moment, it seemed to cast a vicarious smile of approval down upon me, and that was enough for me.

I knelt over her then, steadying myself with one hand on the hilt of my sword and the other pressed against the sooty ooze coating the wet brick wall beside me. As her blood ran down the blade and sank into the earth, she set a terrified gaze directly into my eyes, but it wasn't the terror that comes with regret, it was the terror that comes with finality, the terror that comes with the realization that all of your perceptions were lies. That you were wrong and it was too late to admit it. As I wrenched her pitiful soul from its fleshy prison, she understood. In that moment, the final stone cast, the bargain struck, she understood with total clarity the gravity of the gift, which I had, with pleasure, bestowed upon her. For even though on this night she had barely escaped the demon's grasp, her reckless, dark desires fuelled by the self-loathing would have eventually betrayed her into the arms of another. Of that, the moon and I had no doubt. If the demon wanted her now, he would have to come back and pick at her carcass. I left her there and returned to the shadows from whence I came and where I belonged.

I didn't meet Michael until about a year or so later, and it was Michael—arrogant, pompous, idiotic Michael—who taught me how to laugh again.

I have to smile when I think of him. His was as trite and cliché an existence as one could get, yet his arrogance was refreshing. He wore it with the flair of a circus clown.

He *had* everything that a life of exceptional wealth and privilege could possibly provide, so to expect anything less than an egotist was absurd. Raised in the proper fashions of the social aristocracy, he lived favorably, afforded luxuries well beyond most people's wildest imaginations, and he took it all for granted, because it was expected of him. Oxford awaited, along with a promising business career and the status it would ultimately grant him. But sadly enough, promises made while travelling on the road to disappointment are promises rarely kept. In the end, all the worthless possessions would end up owning him, and a six-figure salary no longer seemed like fair trade for his life. He wanted out, but his entire life had never once been about what he truly wanted. He had obligations—obligations he neither wanted *nor* needed. He made that very clear to me almost immediately, but I think it was my ambivalence that drew him to me. His braggadocio wasn't worth the effort on my part, and yet he had certain glamour about him, an unusual sensitivity that made me take notice. He went on and on and on ad nausea about the limitless supply of fast cars, loose women, and illegal drugs he had at his disposal—well, as much as his parents' money could buy. He abused his privilege like a true and proper scoundrel. "But eventually," he exclaimed as if he had discovered a new philosophy: the thrill of it all didn't seem so thrilling, and one party after another had just blurred into one long non-stop boring debauch for him. He admitted that there was nothing original in his life. His entire persona, as melodramatic as it was, was nothing more than a cheap imitation, and he was right. There was no scandal that hadn't been done better by someone else. I knew the

Marquis, so all I could do was suck my teeth and nod my head at Michael's exaggerations and confabulations.

I had come to Brighton that day for no other reason than to embrace the midnight sea and take in a bit of stargazing. Dance clubs held no attraction for me. Too much static. Too much diluted agony. Cold-filtered chemical and hormone induced hysteria, nothing more. Every emotion negated itself. Nothing was pure. But I had no prospects for the evening, and in a desperate mortal sort of way, I wanted a drink to ease the boredom. Alcohol had absolutely no affect on me, but I liked the taste of it. One takes one's pleasure where they can get it, and I took quite a bit that night with little regard for the goings on around me.

I wouldn't have taken the slightest notice of Michael, but he propositioned me rather confidently as I was leaving the club. Cold as a corpse and equally discontented he asked, "Hey, would you like to go back to my flat for some coke and some interesting sex?"

Interesting sex? I thought. How could anyone in his or her right mind refuse such an enticing and amusing offer? Although the amusement would be entirely mine to enjoy. Having shagged enough rotting corpses, I knew that the sex would be neither enticing nor remotely interesting. But I was intoxicated with the *idea* of something interesting and bored to the point of wanting to slash my own wrists, so the unspoken consideration of my options took less than a fraction of a second.

"Why not?" I replied with a wink of my eye and a sumptuous flirty flick of my hair. It was always too easy.

After a couple of lines of coke and a down-n-dirty shag in the backseat of his convertible, we headed off to his flat. We had the car at one hundred-ten miles per hour when we took it over the cliff, and we howled with laughter the entire way down. Even the whining and the screeching of the metal as it crushed and tore against the rock face of the ravine wasn't enough to drown out the laughter. For Michael, it would be his last laugh, of course. He said he had never flown before and that it was the most *interesting* thing he had done in his life.

And so it went, my life, on an on like the script of a bad horror film where the monster kills the innocence and no one can stop it. I mean really. I have crossed paths with hundreds of faces a year, over thousands of years. Is anyone innocent? I had heard someone say once that some people just *need* killing, and after a few thousand years as witness to the theater macabre that is humanity, I had begun to believe in that need, until Myra. She changed the way I felt about everything…

Sweet child Myra could no longer endure his caress. The advances had begun innocently enough, sitting on his lap—her father's lap. She needed him, adored him, loved him more than anything. He was everything to her, in spite of it all…even the pain.

But the pain was nothing compared to the dark, and as the darkness deepened, she was overcome by such an intense, all-consuming sorrow that she felt deceived, worthless, betrayed, lost, and alone…until the fire. I remember the first time the fire came to me. I remember the heat and the rapture. Yes, the fire became her one and only true friend. It danced for her, warmed her, understood her. Its command soothed and calmed her—calmed her brutalized emotions, cleansed her soul, and destroyed the sense of powerlessness that had contaminated her. In that, I understood her, understood the dank hollow of her soul in as much as the cold blade of hatred and indifference understood my own.

On her sixteenth birthday, I suggested that petrol would offer a most superior burn, and when she asked, I lit the match for her, with pleasure.

Her mother: the sycophant. No, that's not quite right. Her mother: the submissive, narcissistic, self-medicated delusional drama-queen, and her father, the monster, watched in horror, bound to their chairs as the flames stripped the flesh from her bones. They screamed, begged for mercy, begged for forgiveness, pledged eternal devotion, and threw their sins like salt over their shoulders, but it wasn't enough. It would never be enough, and so she spoke not a word to them. Neither a whimper nor a tear did she utter. Such a brave girl to sacrifice her own innocence to make a point. She sought to invoke neither guilt nor shame. Vengeance was all she desired, wishing only to stain their last moments with her anguish.

The blaze seemed to obliterate all the stars in the sky and could be seen well into the next dimension. It burned brightly—so, so brightly—bright as the purity of her soul, and it would light my way until I reached the end of my own personal eternity.

9

Of Art *and Human Wretchedness*

Of all my mortal passions, and I had many, art was always an obsessive fixation for me. I had been afforded the rare privilege of immortality, not something to be taken lightly, and that had allowed me to bear witness to the lives of many a tormented artist as they plodded along down their chosen path. Most of them eventually matured into skilled masters, despite the obstacles, real or imagined. I've seen a lot of suffering, have slogged through too many lifetimes to count, but the suffering of an artist is mania spectacular to behold. So even though the long, dreary, monotonous years of my existence had soured almost all enjoyments, idling in a museum among the haunting spirits of old was my last, truly meaningful indulgence—a minuscule respite from the duty of liberating abandoned souls—and I desperately clung to it.

If it's art you seek, London is ridiculous with galleries. There is such an overabundance of art in London, I could not help but glut on it whenever I so fancied.

Having gallivanted all about the world and back for centuries while attempting to assert themselves as rulers supreme, the English have *collected* a great deal of artworks; though opinions of that term vary greatly, as many would say they surreptitiously appropriated it during conquest, which would make it more pillaging and looting than collecting. But I must allow for some leniency, as they were the first, shall we say, *civilized country,* to endow art galleries and museums a status equivalent to that of libraries as popular resources, not to mention that most galleries are free, so in actuality, they facilitated the availability of culture to the commoner. My recommendation to any commoner is to whet your cultural appetite on classical art and antiquity first, but my advice, I must admit with a grin, is rather prejudiced.

As far as offerings go, London has the standard collection of old world art, from Bosch to Van Eyck, but there is a lot of British art on display as well, from Henry Moore's alluring, almost erotic, sculptures, to Constable's romanticized landscapes, which never fail to stir heart-wrenching longings for the countryside in me. But my personal favorites were Francis Bacon's *grotesque and nightmarish* figurative interpretations of the human psyche, which, however garish and disturbing, were more akin to my spirit.

I am not much for still life, but, if one were so inclined, one might take in some of Samuel Peploe's paintings. His bold use of color, his inclination towards thick and morose backgrounds, and his petulant penchant for robust lighting have afforded him the distinguished title of master. Such complexity of tone and texture, such rustic realism, his works are often said to rival those of the impressionists, though I vehemently disagree with that, but what do I know of still life? For thousands of years I have beheld a world in a constant state of flux and can attest that life is anything but still, so the term seemed like an oxymoron. Inanimate objects in a static setting, to me, certainly do not represent life, figuratively or otherwise.

Now one cannot embark upon any artistic excursion in London without hearing about the Tate Modern. It is, in these circles, the talk of the town and the largest modern art gallery in the world. The austere yet strikingly simplistic lines of the building stand in sharp contrast to its neighbor, Saint Paul's Cathedral, where I often seek solace and beauty and faith. Even so, The Tate really is worth visiting, if only to admire its brutish physique, as I was sadly unimpressed with the so-called art as much as I was unimpressed with its utilitarian coldness. It all seemed so detached and featureless in comparison to the sumptuous depth—the almost liquid temptation—and vivaciousness of the greats: Michelangelo, Botticelli, da Vinci...pay me no mind, I could go on forever. Call me old world, but even after looking upon those tattered canvases for centuries, I never grew the slightest bit weary of them, even if every now and then my palette did crave a bit of variety.

Now I am not an art critic. Let me be clear about that. It was solely for entertainment's sake that I enjoyed attending art gallery openings. "The thrill of discovery," I would declare to anyone who asked. That was the catch phrase I often used to justify my curiosity, but maybe it was simply a mortal attempt to be moved by something, anything at all. One of my choice haunts was the Serpentine in South Kensington, as they have always made it a point to showcase new, up-and-coming British artists, and on one such night of discovery—cool, rainy, worried by mist and biting winds—it was that I met Ian.

As art gallery openings go, this was as awfully passé as one could get. The stench of snobbery masquerading as artistic appreciation was overwhelming, and the subdued lighting and the fancy glassware only assisted in perpetuating the illusion.

Atmosphere aside, the works on display were avant-garde and affecting, to say the least. The intricate details placed against a milieu of stabbing, primitive brush strokes were resplendent, stirring me well beyond all mortal comprehension. The horrifying monstrous figures, with their weeping hateful eyes, bared teeth, and blood-stained claws, pierced through the canvases directly into my soul, revealing to me, for the first time, an obscure reflection of my true self.

As I stood there, sipping my champagne, pondering the implications of my epiphany, a scent, drifting willowy across the room, captured my interest: Fear. The savory stink of carrion. The aroma of sweat and rotting meat rushed over my senses, and my fingertips began to go numb. I moved to the corner of the main room and set my glass down. Back to the crowd, I stared at my own reflection in the mirrors lining the wall. My skin had taken on a sickly greyish hue, my hands were cold now, and the sweet scent of failure seemed as if it were collecting around me in a swirling mist.

Where are you my friend?

Come out, come out, wherever you are.

Sharpening my vision, I turned away from the dreadfulness that was my own face and glanced from one end of the gallery to the other, seeking my quarry with vulturous eyes, and there, yes, there, out of place in the midst of the bloated mass of grotesquely crisp social elitists, was the source of the sweet perfume. He reeked of it: the pungent dew of old death. He exuded it from his every pore, reveled in it, as if he were borne of it.

I can remember thinking what a lean, stringy fucker he was, and how the ill-fitting suit only served to accentuate that fact. His long, scraggy hair fell all over his face with no particular rhyme or reason, and the reflexive, anxious twitching—gazelle-like in its need to seek an escape—punctuated his absurdly awkward elasticized gracefulness. He was but a sweaty, nervous, parody, nothing more at first glance, but definitely worth taking notice of. "Bravo!" I applauded with glee, forgetting myself for moment, but it didn't matter. Everyone else thought I was applauding the painting now in front of me, but I was really applauding the *painter*.

Yes, the artist...I should have known, should have sensed it immediately, as it was blatantly evident that he did not belong among the writhing collection of delusional hypocrites present who chewed their fancy food like cattle, all the while feigning intellectual interest in this and that. No. He belonged to his passion: consumed, loved, and tortured by it. I almost felt pity—almost.

As the hours passed, I watched him reluctantly engage in the trivial conversations of lesser men, every word uttered stabbing into him like red-hot irons. He barely spoke. It was as if he were afraid he would choke on his own unsophisticated words and thoughts. Too bad really, because I was certain that anything he had to say would have been infinitely more stimulating than the bravado being bandied about by the lot of these *nouveau riche* idiot savants. The Inquisition was an orgiastic thrill compared to this. Thankfully and finally, a butler, offering pause to refresh everyone's drinks, presented the escape, and delightfully amusing it was as I watched him scuttle through the crowd then bolt for the rear entrance, arms flailing in some imagined, blustery torrent.

I could just barely contain the laughter as I followed —resolute in my task. However, the comedic intermission was to be a brief one…

Retching, face down in the gutter, stinking of liquor and vomit—crippled by his own mediocrity—was how I found him a few minutes later.

Those of the artistic persuasion are invariably a ragged lot. The tortured artist persona is a beloved stereotype, and suffering is a marketable commodity. But Ian's suffering was neither self-gratifying artifice nor publicity stunt. He was beyond pathetic. Putting him out of his misery would be mercy in the kindest of terms. My sword—at the ready and heavy in my hand—gleamed in the cold fluorescence of the street lamp. It would be quick, for my sake as much as his.

"Sebastian," I hissed gravely as my shadow swallowed up what was left of the light. "Get up!"

I knew he heard me, but he didn't answer. He doubled over and spat the remainder of his partially digested *hors d'oeuvres* into the gutter, and then he looked up at me with the most dazzling crystal-blue eyes I had ever seen, so vulnerable and tender, so considerable in size that they gave his sallow face a lovely, almost chaste quality. I misplaced my thoughts and the steadiness of my legs for an instant. When he finally spoke, I felt a dizzying rush of blood to my head.

"I want to go home," he said, stammering through the spastic heaves as he fell backwards into the lightpost, and at the sound of his voice, so deep and yet so inconspicuous, I lost my train of thought. I do not know where my mind got off to in that moment, but it had left the task-at-hand entirely. His plea for compassion had roused some tiny trace of emotion in me, a remnant of empathy still buried within me that I was unaware even existed, so I suggested a taxi. It was the polite thing to do, I supposed, since killing him was no longer a viable option for the time being, but my kindness was rebuffed with an assertive: "No." accompanied by the explanation that he did not live that far and could walk the distance, to which I countered, "My dear Sebastian…I seriously doubt you have that ability at the present time, and being flip isn't going to help the situation either."

"I don't need your help," came the reply as he declined my offer while pointing out the inaccuracy of my assumption. "And no one except my mum has called me that since birth, my name is Ian."

"Well *Ian*, allow me to retort: I am not trying to help you. It's just that you're ruining the pleasant ambiance of this lovely street with all the retching and drunken nonsense, so let's forgo the innocence and confusion. Just get up and stop acting so damn ridiculous!"

As he staggered to regain his footing, I kindly touched my hand off his elbow, and that's when the innocent confusion left his face. Jaw set hard, he recoiled violently at the gesture, as if I had mauled him in some fashion. I didn't take offense at his rejection. I was well beyond offense, and actually, his asinine stubbornness was quite refreshing. As for whether or not he needed killing, that was a question woefully without an answer, but we had crossed paths. Fate is fate, so I couldn't walk away, wouldn't walk away. "Well Ian, suit yourself then, but I plan on accompanying you, like it or not."

He didn't much like it and quipped a trite "suit your own damn self" as he dusted off his slacks. Then he shot me a rather self-satisfied look and stumbled off on his way, muttering a cloud of incoherent expletives as he went. I know, the belligerent drunk routine didn't really suit him, but caricatures aside, I admired the icy sarcasm employed to shield his pain. His melancholia was magnificent, aged like fine wine. I would have to think on this one a little while, toy around with it a bit. This one had spirit, and a challenge every now and then is the spice of life, at the very least, it's an antidote to the monotony. I thought I had the upper hand. I always did, but this time, neither one of us had any idea of the dire adventure we were about to embark upon.

10

Assumptions *on the Nature of Death*

———————————————————————

I an's flat—a rehabilitated depository—damp, dark, and lofty—was an asylum for shadows, and no measure of electric fuelled illumination could pretend to break the heaviness of the gloom. The furnishings, spare, only exaggerated the enormity of the space. The architecture was that of pragmatic isolation. I felt lost in the dark here, and cold.

Overhead, suspended from the rusted iron pipes, which randomly divided the ceiling, were rows and rows of paintings, the same wicked and hideous masked portraits I had seen earlier at the gallery. It was a remarkable sight. The severity and the hollow emptiness of their gazes overpowered me. It was almost as if the heavens'

seraphic multitudes were glowering down over my
shoulders—watching me—waiting.

"My, my...aren't they unusual and quite beautiful,"
I said followed by a wistful sigh as I craned my neck in
order to take in every gruesome and haunting expression, but Ian's expression was even more haunting. He
seemed a little taken aback by my response, suspicious
even, so I insisted that I wasn't lying to him or having a
laugh on his account, to which he responded by asking,
"Don't they frighten you?" as he tripped over the paint-
covered tarps lining the floor, entangled in the sleeves of
his jacket as if he held match with a serpent.

I really wanted to cross the room and help him extri-
cate himself—his lack of coordination was painfully
embarrassing to watch—but I remembered his refusal on
the street, so I stood my ground and pretended that his
clumsiness wasn't affecting me in any way. "Frighten
me? No, not at all," I told him. "They remind me of a
time when I knew myself...or thought I knew myself.
But that's neither here nor there. Who I am is really of
no importance right now, and not much frightens me
anyway. Except for you. Good Lord, Ian, how have you
not managed to break your own neck? Maybe if you'd
pick up a bit and lay off the liquor you wouldn't have
such trouble navigating the floor."

He just shrugged me off, twisted a few more times
in contorted spasms, and then, finally free of his jacket,
he stumbled over to the cramped, barely functional gal-
ley kitchen. "Drink," he shouted in my general direction,
and then, after retrieving two empty glasses from the
dish rack, he commenced spiraling in circles as though
their purpose had gone completely missing from his

mind. "Well, they frighten me, and I *am* the artist who painted them," he professed while shoving an empty glass towards me, only to retract it, mid-gesture, once its purpose finally came to him. "Sorry—whiskey?"

His smile was pithy and enchanting—if a bit melo-dramatic—and as the subtly of it assaulted me, a vague and disconcerting prickling sensation crept over my flesh. I suddenly felt consumed by a desire to lay my hands upon his face, brush the dark hair from his eyes, and lose myself in his purity. I tried reading his mind, but I could decipher nothing of his thoughts: the gentle force of his will, a force stronger than I am sure even he was aware, obstructed them.

"Whiskey will do just fine," I replied, then thanked him again when he handed me my glass. I sat down at the counter and raised the smoky amber liquid to my lips, but before I could take a sip, he asked what I did for a living, stopping only after he realized he was speaking to a total stranger. The vulnerability he felt blushed lightly over his face, and he looked to the floor for com-posure. I, of course, could not suppress my amusement.

"Selena, my name is Selena, and I divine."

"Well, sure—ok," he said with a self-conscious twinge in his voice. "You're not shy are you, Selena, but as an artist, I would agree with that. You are quite divine, the way the light bends itself around you...it's stunning."

"No, Ian, not *divine* like that. No matter, I thank you for the flattering remark, and to answer your question: I am not shy. Not conceited either, but I meant fortune telling, you know...tarot cards, crystal balls, palm read-ing and the like. I don't make a fortune, that's the irony I suppose, but I do get on all right." I wasn't sure if my *not-entirely-fabricated* career aspirations would sit well with him, but when he exclaimed, "Oh bloody hell! Who cares about the money? It must be very exciting—to know the future," the irony of his statement was not lost on me, and so my reply was dim as I tried to conceal a salty smirk: "For me, yes Ian, it is exciting." The smirk was not meant to be interpreted as an invitation, but, in any event, he leant over the counter towards me with a look of deep-seated exasperation wandering aimlessly over his pallid face.

"I would love to know my fortune—please?"

It was the way he said *please* that intrigued me. With the excitement of a child, he eagerly laid his arm on the counter, palm up, the loose cuffs of his shirt shifting ever so slightly as he extended his arm towards me. How could I refuse? How could I indeed when his outstretched appeal revealed the pale jagged lines of despair, criss-crossing his wrists and forearms?

I seized his hand and pulled it into the light.

He didn't fight it. I don't think he had any life in him to fight. His flesh was cold, so cold to the touch—dry—and sparks of static lit off my fingertips as I guided them over the Braille transcripts of his misery. "Are you not afraid of dying then?" I asked, fixing him with a hardened look directly into his lovely blue eyes, and he met my stare and held it, confidently.

"Even a shameful coward can be brave for the few seconds it takes to kill yourself, and besides, I'm an idealist, so anything's got to be better than this."

His reply was blunt and defiant, despite the self-doubt and the admission of guilt. Suffice it to say, I was not typically at a loss for the proper words. However, being forced to dispense with this significantly rude awakening had my stomach twisting into knots. "Well, Ian…what good is it to know your future if you couldn't care less, and more importantly, I think that you might have been misinformed regarding the nature of death. Something does exist beyond life, I have seen it, have walked with the shadows, and there lies terror so profound, horror so unspeakable, and anguish beyond all measure. No. You would derive no comfort from this *death* you seek, and your soul would survive insufferable torment only to live on, regretting it for an eternity." His shoulders slacked as disappointment gripped him. "I know, Ian," I continued, "The truth is a lot to take in at once."

"That's not it…," he replied with a slight stammer and a pause to pull his hand from my grasp as if he were ashamed of its disclosure. "I just wanted to feel—"

"Worthy?" I asked, finishing his sentence. I knew that I had again taken liberty with my assumption, but it seemed like the fitting end to his thought. It wasn't. It was a grievous error, and he countered in a pained and tearful, almost inaudible whisper:

"Significant," he said with shoulders hunched so far forward it appeared as though he were trying to fold up into himself.

Yes. Significant? It's an interesting word, often has that effect on people, and upon reflection, I concluded that it was also a telling word, but it was the tears that caught me off guard. I have only rarely been accosted by tears. I know that doesn't seem possible, but as a rule, the dispatching of a soul is seen to expeditiously so as to avoid any begging for mercy or other such complications, like tears. Tears have always caused me a great deal of discomfort. I lack the social skills and graces to deal with them, not to mention that I lack the stomach for it as well. Tears imply regret. He who regrets will never be free from bondage.

I could taste the salt in the air, and although Ian's future escaped me—my considerable talents aside—I felt an intense necessity to offer him his truth, even if it would be nothing more than a meager comfort to him: "You will be significant…that is your future, my sweet Sebastian, for whatever it's worth."

Eventually, Ian took leave of his consciousness, his body so weakened from the liquor and the grief. Meantime, amid the cruel hours of the twilight—infuriated to such a considerable degree by his sorrow—I willfully stalked the faint-lit streets, forsaking sleep, as it could offer no solace to my rotted soul nor give any ease to my agitated mind.

I don't recommend wandering the phantasma. The late hours of darkness brim with evil, and the shadows conjure up the filthiest, repugnant dredges of society. Vile fiends they are, speaking with hushed breaths in the gloaming. Everywhere they surround me—the walking dead—victims, the entire lot of them, victims of their idiosyncratic aberrations. Precariously they live, lacking the courage of their convictions: convictions based on dogma so tenuous, the mere utterance of a contradictory opinion could raze its foundations to the ground. To live so is absurdity, but they do, enslaved by fear and gluttonous desire—wanting—always wanting for something more, something better, while living in fear that that want will go unfulfilled. That want makes them smutty, wretched, and ungrateful creatures, contentedly wallowing in the stink of their own desperation.

So I declared to the Cosmos that if it was despair, wantonness, and fear that humanity desired then they would have it—have it all. They would have it in all its wondrous subtleties, its monstrous glory, and its sickening depravity. They would have my wrath—beg for it—for that was all they were worth.

Possessing a renewed clarity of intent, and so as not to be remiss again in my duties as I had earlier, I would unleash a reprisal of unspeakable magnitude. Night after night, the streets, the alleyways, and all the secluded corners of London would run red as the coming of the dawn drew nigh, and no matter where you chose to hide, I would find you, if I wanted to...and I did...want, and it was a heinous wanting, a blackened wanting—pitch black to its core.

I would hack and slash and burn my way through cartilage and bone until the blade of my sword was left dull with impunity. I slaughtered thousands for no other reason than they begged me not to, but eventually, even a death dealer of my tenure grows bored. I was content with the fact that I had executed my duty justly, that my hate had been genuine and potent, so I took pause from the carnage to salvage a small moment of calmness and contemplate the splendor of the sunrise. Its ruddy splinters pierced the tranquil indigo of the dawning sky and flushed tenderly over my hands—gnarled hands—stained to the very bone with the blood of complacency.

Several months of blood-soaked moons and miraculous sunrises I would applaud with wonderment before the thousand years of solitude wore away at the stoic pretense I wore like armor, and I expectedly returned to Ian.

Not having within my grasp suitable words of apology, I remained penitent and oddly silent as he stood, arms crossed tight over his chest, his foot tap, tap, tapping the floor as he leant against the massive iron door of his flat. "I hoped that you would come back," he confessed while exhaling a lengthy, impassioned, albeit a nervous sigh of relief, but when he asked, "What took you so long?" the impish smile and the scolding twinkle in his eye left me utterly defeated. There was no hope but to find my words…

"I am so sorry, Ian. It was dark, and I lost my way."

11

Sentiment *and Sensibility*

Talking with Ian was a most enjoyable exercise in glibness; although, every now and again, he would let his guard down, extending a sinister invitation into his world...one that I enthusiastically accepted.

His was a modest, happy, and uneventful childhood, he said. Born in Swindon, his parents—a schoolmistress and a registrar—kind and decent folk of moderate disposition, had the highest of aspirations for their only child. They cherished him more than life itself and doted on him to excess, with much energy focused on indulging his every childhood whim. Spoiled, maybe, but life was idyllic and simple for the pig-hill lad. All his hopes and dreams were within reach, until a darkness so immeasurable descended upon him. You see, at the ungainly and insufferable age of thirteen, our Sebastian began to suffer erratic black-out seizures, and coincidentally, it was then that the dreadful masked horrors commenced assaulting his dreams. Whether awake or asleep, they whispered to him—sweetly, seductively—twisting the fantasies of his brittle mind into nightmares that rivaled the tortures of a mediaeval witch trial.

His parents, bewildered by the state of affairs, sought remedy for their dearly beloved child in all of the pre-eminent psychiatric facilities in the country, but psychoanalysis is no substitute for faith. His mother often wept into her tea, decrying that "God has forsaken us," and that Sebastian, "is not my son...that demon is not my son." His father had no pride left to swallow. He devoutly believed in the sins of the father: there was no washing his hands of it, so he often fell to his knees and wrapped his arms around his wife's legs in a futile attempt to assuage her hysteria with his own shame.

Neither of them was to blame; however, permit me to add here that, in my experience with medical doctors, their diagnostic skills—in spite of the so-called training and all the Freud reading—are speculative, at best. It was no different for Ian than it had been for me: the anguish he would suffer under the guise of *therapy* would tear his fragile psyche to pieces. Each course of treatment forced upon him drove another nail into his mind until absolutely nothing remained, nothing but a cadaverous shell of a man—frail and frightened—unable to deal with even the most trifling of emotions. The prescriptions, without which he couldn't survive, littered every corner of the flat: Clozapine, Haldol, Thorazine. The pharmacology guidebooks state that these rather benign looking tablets supposedly lessen the psychotic improprieties of schizophrenia, thus allowing the patient (i.e. the victim) to function effectively and more importantly, function appropriately, but it was rubbish, all of it. Function appropriately like what? The bloody walking dead—that's what!

Faculties lost in the medicated haze, all of the hopes that Ian might have had diminished into nothing more than stagnant imaginings. There would be no prestigious law school, nor any type of school whatsoever, and after an endless sequence of demeaning factory jobs, he left home, admittedly crushed by the unbearable disappointment. Upon moving to London, he managed to obtain part-time work cleaning the toilets of the famed British Museum, and although he knew in his heart that the job was beneath him and that he had been cheated out of a life, the hush of the museum was abundantly therapeutic, in that, he said it was the only remaining place he could manage to achieve peace from the madness festering in his mind.

So despite the career inclination to immerse himself in sewage, the splendor of the museum was not mislaid upon him. Alone, in the small hours just before dawn, he would pace the hallowed marble halls, his loneliness echoed in vacant footsteps, hearkened only to the spirits imprisoned within the paintings. Isolated from the world by the darkness, it was in those profoundly desolate hours that he fell in love, in love with the shimmering fluency of the paint. How it spoke to him in the dark, obliterating the pain as it blend it away within its sensual, sublime strokes. In that divine medium, Ian would endeavor to release the demons from his mind and hold them bound to the canvases that he wrought.

He turned out to be a good painter. A rare talent, in fact, and in due course, Ian's robust enthusiasm manifested into a passion of such extreme intensity that it destroyed utterly all of his crippling awkwardness. As if a miracle had set him free from the shackles of apprehension and insecurity, Ian's clumsy gesticulations transformed into the graceful, almost balletic aria of some preternatural being—a melody of rhythm and movement cavorting audaciously with the gentle shifts of alternate times and dimensions.

Spellbound, not unlike a serpent bewitched by the charmer's sway, I was—regrettably.

I spent the majority of my days whiling away the hours enraptured by Ian's brow-furrowing endurance. The demons stood very little chance against such determination. His aura shone luminous as he cleaved the spirits from his mind and thrust them onto the barren canvases with assured, yet savagely brutal strokes. He had grown well beyond their power: purpose and perseverance had replaced fear of failure and anxiety, and their hold upon him was weakening.

Over time, our platonic acquaintance evolved and matured into great admiration and respect for each other, maybe even love, but I could not be entirely certain as to the nature of the emotions stirring within me.

The minutes to hours and the days to months slipped effortlessly away into years of contentment.

Immersed feverishly in his artistic labors, Ian barely noticed the routine movements of the world, so I, decid-

edly, made it my sole devoted duty to bring that world
to him. With the advent of modern technologies, there
was very little that one could not procure directly from
the comfort of one's own home, if money were no object.
For me, money had never been a bone of contention or
any other sort of object. Compliance and commitment to
duty had always provided for my needs, meager as they
were. I *needed* nothing. I wanted for nothing, neither
food nor shelter, comfort nor rest. I had more money
than one need ever accumulate, so from time to time I
would shower Ian with a flux of tantalizing delights:
arcane texts and mystical spell-books, alchemical brews
and potions, textiles of the finest silken fibers, wine, an-
tiquities, and a limitless supply of rare and exotic
pigments, any of which could have inspired the Gods.

All of this errant bric-a-brac, alongside Ian's countless paintings, slowly transformed the flat into the finest
collection of art and antiquity anyone could ever have
wanted to possess. I was confident, judging by the tragi-
cally amusing and utterly ridiculous toothy smile fixed
upon his face, that he was most pleased.

On occasion, in between the lavish and excessive
doting, my exhaustive necromantic studies, and Ian's
ceaseless whiles of creation, we would take a rather
spontaneous fancy to a number of society's more digni-
fied cultural offerings. We travelled often, visiting every
museum and opera house in the whole of the world. I
had been all over the known world already, but somehow, seeing the wonders of the world through the eyes
of such a disarmingly naive companion made it all seem
new and exciting again. I felt connected to something
beyond myself, beyond the monster I had become. I

hadn't even claimed a soul in years. It wasn't that I no longer felt the suffering or that I no longer struggled with my existential thoughts on loyalty, divinity, and the plight of humankind. I did suffer and struggle—with my unrequited feelings for Ian and the knowledge that destiny is never without sacrifice.

Reservations notwithstanding, after many of our prolonged and somewhat dreamy sojourns, Ian's sensibilities would oftentimes run astray, and he would, unconsciously so, slightly overstep the boundaries of our relationship. On this one particular night, I opted not to force a correction...

12

Fear or Death

Please forgive me, well, forgive this rather abrupt and bold suggestion..., Ian asked while shifting his feet as if he had misplaced his command of balance and his sense of propriety. "I would like to paint your portrait, Selena. If you wouldn't mind terribly."

Now the offer posed, though flattering, revealed the constant and innocent nature of his feelings towards me as they resisted all his futile attempts at concealment. He just stood there, shifting aimlessly from one foot to the next, staring and picking at his calloused fingers, and my own feelings, oddly beyond my control, had become muddled in the moment. I wanted to possess him. I *wanted* to make passionate love to him, if only to keep alive what little humanity remained in me, but as I began to cast off my clothes for the portrait, his expression changed. It became tainted of fear mingled with an unexpected hint of dazed bewilderment. His eyes grew into great blue tearful oceans, and his lower lip paled and trembled when he asked, "What are you doing, Selena… that's not necessary?"

The nervousness in his voice prompted me to tread lightly. I was trying to seduce him and apparently not having a great deal of success with the endeavor, but all I could manage to say was, "Don't worry, Ian, I gave up any shred of modesty centuries ago…and this is what you want, isn't it?"

Apparently it wasn't. He whispered a shameful *yes*, then shouted a very dramatic *NO*, then he attempted to negate his anger with a softer *no* until finally admitting, "Shit, Selena, I don't know what I mean. I simply want to paint your portrait."

Simply paint my portrait? Again, it was the way he said it: *Simply.* He said it as if he were unaffected by my presence, as if our relationship were free of deceit. Nothing was further from the truth. "Nothing is ever simple, Ian, and why would you want to do that, so you can imprison my soul as well? Take care now, good sir, the waters might be muddy, but I can still make out the depraved desires hidden in the recesses of *your* mind."

He had barely a reply, nothing more than an "I can't," which came stuttering out of his mouth as he continued his slow and steady backward stride.

"Can't? Can't what, Ian? Can't get close to anyone unless they are covered in paint? Why on earth not? Are you impotent? Are you afraid of naked flesh? The scent of sex, maybe? Or are you afraid of me?"

"I'm afraid of everything, Selena, you know that, and I feel as if I am not on solid ground with you."

His reasoning was tactless and completely idiotic. So enraged I was that my hands clenched, sending talons of antipathy biting into the flesh of my palms. I felt the need to taunt him mercilessly, so I asked, "When is anyone ever on solid ground?" And he seemed at a loss for words when I pointed to the ground beneath his feet. "It teems with vipers, scorpions, and every foul thing you can imagine. You can't tell where you end and where they begin, and they can pick your bones clean, so one should take care never to walk about barefoot and oblivious, but that doesn't mean it's acceptable to take a defeatist attitude. A life caged by one's own shadow? It seems death might be the wiser alternative...would you not say? Fear or Death, Ian? What's it to be then, luv?"

"That's damnation, not choice, Selena, and how many times do you think I've tried to choose? For fuck' sake, what do you know of my pain, anyway? Nothing! *You* **can't** *feel* anything, and you have no idea how dark my shadow can be."

"I wouldn't be so certain of that," I shot back, full of venom. "What is it going to take to get through to you, Ian? It's not about what I feel; it's about what I understand. It's about what *you* feel. Why would you ever want to cast your life away like so much refuse? Have you ever once stopped to acknowledge that the choice of life or death was never yours to make in the first place? Have you ever once thought that in all of the realms of possibility maybe a greater purpose awaits you?" I felt the contempt start to burn through my veins. I felt my own shadow, eerily at ease and detached, fill the room like a dark dragon emerging from the confines of its lair. A foul and nameless beast, it cast its pestilent silhouette over all in its path as my voice bellowed with hatred. "No, of course not. You don't think of these things because you're a coward, *Ian*. You're not man enough to master the gifts that you have been so generously awarded. You haven't the remotest idea of the power you possess, its absolute grandeur withered and wasted —wasted on your arrogant, self-deprecating attitude! I should have killed you the night we met. Should have slit your throat, shined my boots with your blood, and left your carcass to rot in the street."

Ian cowered away, weak, terrified, and confused. The sweat beaded upon his skin, glistening like a thousand tiny diamonds, and the wraiths, no longer seeking asylum in the periphery of his demented world, animated into crazed, blackened, feculent caricatures. They cackled in amusement, swung from the rafters, and pointed elongated bony fingers at their mad puppeteer.

Light-headed, unable to take the depth of breath needed to stave off the panic, Ian thrashed about the place, knocking over everything in his wake as he grasped savagely for some minute semblance of control. In the corner of the room, the flame from an upended candle set a pool of spilled thinner on fire as the gaunt, spidery shadows descended upon him in a crawling mass of darkness, clawing at what was left if his sanity.

I stood there and watched the fire spread across the steaming, squirming floor, watched it catch on the black velvet fabric hanging across the window. Watched the fire consume it in a flash of hot ash and smoke as it burned a path of protest towards the ceiling. It would only be a moment before those horrid paintings were charred to oblivion, but I had grown weary and bored with watching the second-rate theatrics. I was over and done with all of the subtle maneuverings and the trite, unfashionable scheming. Trepidation and limitation—best enjoyed by the eternally damned—would be Ian's ruin now. I walked through the smoke and flame, grabbed him by the collar of his shirt, spun him around, and shoved him backwards. My shadow followed, collecting soot and hot ash from the air as it moved to take over in my stead. Pinning him to the wall, it rasped against his body to some ungodly-sinful, libidinous rhythm, paralyzing him, and the scorch of the dragon's breath set him to faint.

While my shadow had his undivided attention, I lifted a butcher's knife from its sheath on the kitchen counter, walked over, and held it out to him. "Do it, Ian, if death is what you truly desire. If a coward can, in fact, be brave, then take up the knife. Do it now. Liberate yourself." Those words, full of bitterness and fury, I spat in his face, singeing his meager fortitude to its puny, rotted core. I grabbed his wrist and placed the knife into his hand—its broad blade, shiny, slick, and cool to the touch. "Do it, Ian…save me the trouble. For once, be the master of your own destiny and do it now."

The first cut, easing fluently through the flesh, was feeble at best. I had hoped for a more zealous attempt, but I should have set my expectations slightly lower. He, like all the others, lacked the courage of his convictions. He, like all the others, needed some gentle convincing.

"Deeper, Ian," I commanded as his blood ran, quick and thickly, onto the wooden floorboards beneath his bare feet. It didn't even look like blood. It looked thin and faded like the thousand other paint splatters that now permanently stained the floor, but it didn't matter, the sacrifice, however insignificant, warmed my soul to its center, so while smiling with immense satisfaction, I leant into his ear, and with lips lightly grazing the soft skin of his cheek, I whispered, "Now, Ian, the other one."

Resigned to the pointlessness of any struggle, he, of course, obeyed, sawing at his wrists with a newly found, crazed vigor. Tendons snapped, their rubbery tone reverberating throughout the silence of the room, and a deluge of blood and poison issued forth with such force that the knife dropped from his grasp, bounced off the floor once, and then slid in a spin to finally rest at my feet. I picked it up and wiped the greasy rusted-out blade on my trousers while Ian just stared at his wrists—hypnotized—scrutinizing his handiwork, which was now nothing more than an oozing mass of mangled meat. Eventually, he fell backwards onto the sofa—contented—the demons satisfactorily exorcised, I supposed.

He was at peace, for the first time in his life, and therein lay the irony: there wasn't much time left for him. His wounds wept a sorrow I could barely bear to look upon. I sat astride his emaciated torso, clenched his flaccid wrists in my hands to quell their angry issuance, and looked into his eyes—hollow eyes. The eyes of a dead man. There was nothing to see but an endless emptiness, and I could smell the surrender on his flesh: soft and sweet, like the scent of honey in the sun on a warm day. I snaked my tongue up along his throat and over his chin.

When I found his mouth, still and cold, I closed my lips over his. I could taste the vital force eeling away from his body, and finally, through a half-lidded gaze, his soul—rent and tortured—moved into my line of sight. Engulfed in a languid, semi-conscious euphoria, it struggled for its freedom.

I could have released him right then and there, by all accounts, I should have. I should have snatched his soul from his flesh and been done with the whole sorry affair, but something stayed my hand. I saw something, felt something, and it wasn't mercy. His soul thrashed about in a wild fever, but it was not a struggle for freedom. No. My first impression was in error. The desperation was much more severe, more acute. It didn't feel the futility of its own struggle. It didn't want freedom. It wanted something so much more elusive than that, something I had wanted once…a long time ago, and so instead of releasing him from his sin, I released him from his desire: because he was a damn fool. He could not see that death was never his decision. "It was always mine, Ian, and now is not the time." I gently pushed his eyelids closed, checked his wrists to be sure the wounds had sealed, and then I watched…and waited.

Countless lonesome hours passed quietly into the twilight, as I stood, watching over Ian—watching as sleep's sweet languor cradled him and spirited him away into some tranquil solitude—a solitude untainted and innocent, fraught only with blissfully untroubled moments, far and away from the shadows' expectant bony claws.

How I longed to journey into that solitude myself, as the centuries of exhaustion had finally strained my being to the point of collapse, so I gently pushed my mind into his. I don't know what I thought I would find there. A manic mind is no place to seek solace, unless of course madness brings you peace. All I can say for sure is that I was inexplicably drawn in, and barely a breath had escaped my lips before the vibrant and erotic bombardment of celestial metaphors had overflowed my subconscious. It was not long until I succumbed to the dulcet dreams of Ian.

DAYS LATER, Ian awakened in a fever, drenched in sweat and fear, just as he had all the mornings of his entire life. Shuddering at the insignificance of the past and trembling at the inevitabilities of the future, he tried desperately to discredit all of the things he had witnessed and foreseen in his tormented dreams. By the time I got to him, he was screaming.

"Ian...it was a dream," I said while putting my arm around him and then squeezing his shoulders into mine. "You just had a bad dream, that's all...everything is going to be all right."

He pushed away from me and curled up tightly in the corner of the sofa, his eyes rounded with bewilderment, his hands wringing at his wrists. "It was real, Selena. *The dragon.* I saw the fire dragon, and I was bleeding. *My wrists.* They were shredded to bits. It felt like...like I was dying, all twisted together with the snakes and the scorpions, the shadows and the demons, but then I was soaring over barren, ancient lands. *The wind.* The unbearable wind and the sand biting at my face. Selena, if it wasn't real, how is it that I can remember so clearly places that I have never been, places so ravaged by time and decay that I could never have been?"

I knew what he was asking. I had been adrift in his mind when he crossed over, so if there were ever a more appropriate time for me to find the proper words, it was now: "Ian…what you have experienced, it is described as *drifting the mysteries*, where by one can, via an astral projection of the mind, travel through the fabric of time by employing the avenue of dreams. This ability, or gift, it is beyond all logical reasoning, beyond the tedium and the banality of the rational world entirely. Many are blessed with this gift. Some choose to refute it, and others, well…others embrace it. A great man, a man I once called friend, a man who understood what exists within and beyond the shadows once wrote to me and said: 'Those who dream by day are cognizant of many things, which escape those who dream only by night, and all that we see or seem is but a dream within a dream.'" But Ian did not understand. He said as much in a feeble whisper with his palms pressed to his temples, fingers entangled, wrenching at clumps of his panic-soaked hair, and his eyes, his eyes were red and swollen with tears of frustration and despair. "You resist it, Ian," I continued, trying to lend a sense of calm to my voice. "And so you fail to understand it. All those drugs have dimmed your wits, and it's a little too late for tears. Your entire life you have feared your gift and not an innate fear either but a learned fear, dictated by your parents and societal tenets. You could see in the dark, and so they labeled you a freak. You believed it—they made you believe it. You have barely lived, hoping that death would somehow release you from your fear of yourself, but death has been elusive for you because it is not in the Universe's design.

"You need to embrace the Universe and its chaos and live now as if it matters. It wasn't a dragon, Ian; it was a winged serpent. You need to embrace *it*, and yes, it's true enough that the death the serpent brings it is not the death that you so ignorantly wish to embrace. It is a death more powerful than the corruption of the flesh. The undoing of your physical being has no significance here. To give up everything, to give up what you have always believed to be real, to offer your soul as sacrifice for a higher purpose...that is a difficult choice to make, or more precisely, it is the conscious choice which leads us to rebirth, leads us back to the beginning, where the Cosmos calls to us from the abyss, beckons us, offers us a release from our pain.

"Yes, Ian, it is this glorious choice, the choice to turn away from the wanting, where we may, if we have properly prepared and are true and worthy, choose the manner of our reawakening. When confronted with death in this manner, we may then, and only then, shed our fears, reject all ideals, discard the parts of ourselves that are useless, and choose to live for our purpose. The Serpent has come for you, just like it came for me long ago."

"So I'm not crazy," he replied with a sigh just shy of relief. "And the visions are not the efforts of some mad devil in my brain."

"Of course not, Ian. Your mother was speaking from fear. The devil does not exist, and to attempt to placate your mind with that sort of misguided mythology is a fruitless endeavor. If you were of another time, you would have been revered as a God or burned as a witch. Either way, it would have been the will of the Universe, the pure chaos of it.

"The order of this world is nothing more than illusion. It's all just idle fantasy and self-imposed delusion through restraint and mindless dogmatic devotion. When one embraces the Universe's will and knows, truly knows and understands its power, one can then move beyond the realm of dreams. Only then can we realize the freedom of who we really are, freedom from regret."

His face softened a bit, and his body relaxed as if his soul had finally found the lifeline it sought. He told me that he so desperately wanted that freedom. He begged me to help him, said that I had to help him, or he would surely die by his own hand if need be. "I don't want to dwell in this bloody wretched existence, anymore."

"As you wish, Ian. It's not too late...it's never too late. Never too late to beg for mercy."

And so arose the dawning of our love, as it was at that very moment we would begin a decade of teachings, with a stout sword to strengthen his body and a will to focus his mind.

I had my doubts, but it turned out that Ian was an extraordinarily attentive student. His unbending inclination to effect change was astonishing, and as his newfound confidence flourished, the many grand and terrifying subtleties of his power began to emerge— emerge like the *dragon* he was born to be. He needed only to fancy it, and lo, the skies grew menacing, grey, impenetrable, and heavy with clouds. Casting lightning downward from the heavens, his thoughts cleaved the sky with thunderbolts of the fiercest measure ever beheld in all of time. His power was dazzling. Not since Lucius had I ever met another so alone. In the long unnatural years of my life, I had never met a soul so starved and yet so strong—a soul so like my own.

Endless hours we spent, minds and bodies locked together in a silent, spiraling discourse that would have propelled a rational mind to the brink of insanity. Unwittingly, he had already passed through great distances, much farther than I had ever expected. He needed nothing of my power. He needed only my guidance, ruthless as it was.

Our exalted sojourns into the netherworld thrust upon us the vivid reflections of a mythos beyond the mortal realm, a millennia of ruined and lost lands so richly detailed it was hard to believe they were just the remnants of a memory. Overwhelmed I was at the beauty of those lands and of their peoples as I stood a mere witness through his mind's eye. And equally astonished was he by the boundless mysteries, the apocalyptic truths, and the dizzying marvels that I came to share with him along the way as we travelled backwards and forwards in time down the excessive lengths of barren roads, through sewerous barter towns, glittering megalithic cities, and reeking slums.

We lost ourselves in the morning dew as we laid our naked bodies across the verdant grasslands of the steppe. We gave our souls up to the omnipotent tranquility of the sky, lost our will to breathe atop the peaks of lofty ice-bound mountains, and drown our misgivings in the cool water as we sank to the depths of the sea.

Over the misery-scorched sands of time, we walked together, hand in hand. Walked the dark and lonely path of truth and knowledge. Shrouded in mystery, we walked the shadows between the lands of the living and the lands of dead. Blinded by our own innocence, we walked barefoot towards the sun.

We bore the burden of our sorrow and walked the Cosmos, all for the will of the Gods. And so the years passed. What a wonderful dream it was.

13

Broken I fell, *into the Dream…*

N ever was there a worse night: my every limb was without sensation. In conceding to Ian's artistic requests, the portrait had bound me to this dreadful pose for months. I was beginning to impart the countenance of a stone statue. My demeanor was understandably rancorous, and I was too emotionally and physically exhausted to file down the sharp edges.

Fraught with delirium, Ian took no notice whatsoever of the scowl I had set about to assault him with. He paced fitfully to and fro across the vast expanse of the flat, shaking his head in frustration—a frustration so great that it had spawned a fierce storm, and with it, a deluge of rain and lightning strikes so relentless that they had relieved us of all modes of illumination, save the hearth fire and a few measly candles.

Now I could well appreciate the humble warmth of the fire's glow, as it cast such a heady rouge over everything. One might just faint merely from the romance of it all. Ian, however, would have none of it. Face flushed with rage, hair in a preposterous state of disarray, anxiety pouring down his cheeks in a translucent flood of arbitrary emotion, he looked absurd, and I couldn't resist the temptation to make note of it: "Ian, look at yourself. You have all the charm and decorum of a raving lunatic. It's exhausting just watching you."

"No. What? No, Selena. You're distracting me. It's all wrong, don't you see!" he replied with an arm flailing hysterical fervor that almost bordered on a panic attack. "I don't see you like this. Not at all, damn it. It's so difficult in this light. Its shadows toy with me. They mock me with their insolence...and the paint—it's too thick, the colors look like mud and vomit. No. It's just not right!" He placed his paintbrushes and palette down dismissively, walked over, and then knelt down in front of the divan on which I lay. "The amulet, Selena, it catches the lightning flashes and blurs my vision. It's beautiful, and it suits you, but can't we remove it?"

I responded with a very blunt: No, and left it at that.

"I don't understand, Selena...what's the problem?"

"There is no problem, and I am not deliberately aiming to be difficult, but the fact of the matter is: I have never tried to remove it, and I don't think I can."

"Yes, I know all that, Selena, the amulet was given to you—a gift of love—yes, yes, and yes, you have stated as much, many times, but I still don't see—"

"No *buts*, Ian, your intimate acquaintance with the details is limited, and so I don't expect you to fully understand. All I can say is that I betrayed that love, and this is the only reminder I have of it. My soul resides within, withering away to dust, and my only release from it will be death, I fear. I have nothing further to say on the matter, and you should let it alone."

He reached towards me and took the amulet into the paint-covered palm of his hand. His hand was shaking.

"I can see your soul in this, Selena…the glare from it is blinding, even if *you* have forsaken it."

"You're too affected by sentiment. You see what you want to see, Ian. It's an optical illusion. You see *the me* I discarded long ago. It's just a trick of the light. You see fiction in that light, the machinations of a well constructed fiction, nothing more."

"No, Selena, that is *not* what I see…not what I see at all. Your eyes look of jet in the moonlight, always. This despair you carry around with you has consumed you."

"Ian please, your sincerity is an irritating provocation: violating, nauseating, and I am so tired." I would have done anything to be free of that pose and the pointless discussion. I suggested that we should maybe take a break, or maybe try a different position. If not this way, then I needed him to tell me what it was that he needed, and I would make it so. "Ian…," I asked with a little less condemnation in my voice. "How is it that you see me then?" But he didn't respond, so I spoke his name again, and yet again I got nothing.

There was but an endless nothing.

My words couldn't possibly have reached their mark.

Ian was lost. A formless abstraction had overspread his face, the silence and the nothing had taken hold, and as he stared at the amulet, his eyes shone like mirrored portals, reflecting the depths of some infinite unknown. An unsettling stillness moved over the room, and then suddenly, as if coming out of trance, he made a start, soft as poetry on summer's eve: "I can see you, Selena...so damaged and so frail. I see you lying on a bed of silken fabric, the colors against your skin are so muted, and you are surrounded by walls of white marble and mosaics. The iridescent reflection of a dimming shadow, you lie languishing amid luxury and debasement. You don't belong to it, but it suits you all the same...and your hair, it's glistening like filaments of spun gold in the light of an immense fire."

I felt a penetrating coldness sweep over me, and I shivered as if someone had just walked over my metaphorical grave. I was astonished by the clarity of his vision. How could he see my soul so clearly when I only ever felt its gasping breath?

He stood up, moved behind me—calm and self-assured—and while brushing away the wild tangles of hair that framed the amulet against my heaving chest, he exposed my shoulder, allowing his fingers to linger evocatively against the bare, pale skin of my neck. I reached up and touched that hand, knitted my fingers through his. "Yes, Ian, tell me how you see me."

"I can smell the incense," he continued, his eyes focused away on a horizon far into the nothingness. "It lingers thickly in the air and dusts your flesh with the seductive scent of depravity. Your arm is held out towards the fire, the tips of your fingers reaching off into the distance. You're beckoning to someone with such intense passion and love in your eyes. It almost seems as if you're beckoning to me. But it's not me, is it Selena?

"Your heart laments…but it's not me your heart calls out to." Ian paused for a moment waiting for me to answer his question. I knew whom my heart had called out to. It was Lucius, and the regret that had long ago hardened my heart almost fell from my lips along with his name, but the breath of it caught in my throat when Ian touched me. He leant in and cupped my face in his other hand, his thumb caressing my cheekbone as he reluctantly confessed his anger. "That passion, Selena…all I have ever seen in you and that damnable amulet is that passion. It is the will that shaped your destiny; it is the strength in your sword arm. It is a passion I will *never* possess, and it's the same passion that beckons to me now. I want it, Selena, and I will have it. I must have it." He punctuated his demand by lifting my chin so he could look directly into my eyes. It was the first time our eyes had met in months—his, the palest crystal blue, clear blue like that of the skies, rifting the mountains of my homeland—and I couldn't help but stumble into them. I felt a faint fear of falling, but I didn't want to turn away, so I just closed my eyes instead. I felt him move in closer to me. Could taste his breath: sweet, heated, and so strangely familiar. Then without warning, he pressed his lips to mine so we wouldn't have to speak the lies aloud. We had become victims of our own denials, so we censored each other with kisses: deep kisses, wet kisses, hour-long explorations of rage and tenderness, paced by hurried breaths and the quickened rhythm of our hearts.

For an instant, nothing existed except the wet of his

lips, and while drifting aimlessly on the swell of urgent
desire that now consumed my every thought, my mind
fell away from me. Would Ian be the first to triumph
over the all-encompassing hatred, which for thousands
of years had protected the deserted place I had so named
my heart?

Perhaps…

Perhaps he would…if I could, only allow him to, but
the argument was purely hypothetical and meaningless
the moment he abruptly withdrew from my lips. "Not
here, Selena. Not like this. This might sound demanding
in a desperate sort of way, but I can't deal with you
properly like this. I don't know how. We have to lie
down now. Come with me. Please. Come now, Selena.
Don't force me to beg." So I took his hand, and he led
me across the room where we settled ourselves on the
floor in front of the fire, the heavy canvas drop cloth
creased and crinkled beneath our bodies. For long moments, we said nothing. We just lay together ensconced
in an acre of dried paint and heartbreak—Ian braced
above me, his eyes serene with expectancy…and hope.

I had forgotten what hope looked like, had forgotten
the soft and consuming nature of it. Its enchantments
were as persuasive as my own: even the coldest and
most cynical of hearts could believe, and the longer I
stared into it, the more I began to believe.

I reached up and brushed the loose hair from his
face, and it was at that moment I found myself utterly
lost, lost and falling like a stone into the cloudless blue
of those eyes as endless years of thoughts and emotions
crowded in to ransack my mind. Unable to cobble together a coherent thought let alone speak it, I lifted my

knee and settled my leg over his hip. The invitation—
explicit—set him to trembling, as it was, no doubt, an
emphatic confirmation of his potency. It was the *yes* I
had always wanted to say, the *yes* I had always been unable to say.

As lingering hours passed, the candle flames flashed
and flickered against waves of unsteady breath, and the
fire swelled and soared, fueled by despair and darkness.
Dancing embers flittered about the room and then
dimmed to a lustrous glow as we slid effortlessly into
one another, our bodies and minds held powerless by
the hypnotic sway of desire's rhythm.

I could feel the tremor building between us. I felt it
as an ache deep within the marrow of my bones, and
yes, I loved the cruelty of it. How long I had waited to
feel the passion of a man's soul again, to feel a man's
lust, a man's desperation, and a man's uncompromising
insistence, and as our shadows circled around, through,
and against each other's, Ian's breath quickened. I felt
the wanting in it, felt the heat of it on my skin. So enraptured by every subtle nuance of the act, so attentive to
the pleasure he felt, Ian had lost all conscious awareness.
His brow fell forward and rested gently against mine as
loose tangles of his hair fell over my face.

So soft and flirtatious those unruly tangles of hair.
Their innocence enticed me. Commanded me. And so I
caressed his face and showered his lips with a wantonness I never knew I was capable of, and with each kiss,
with each slick caress, and with each brutal thrust, my
mind overflowed with a confusion of words—imprisoned
words—words that, despite my aberrant hostility and
my icy resolve, would no longer be caged by reason.

They fell softly from tongue to lip, from darkness to light: "I love you my sweet ill-fated Sebastian," I said with all the earnestness of a confession, "Always. I have always loved you, since the day we met, with all that I am and all that I ever was."

I suspected in my delirium that I might have been speaking in tongues, but even though the underlying intent seemed foreign to me, I knew that I meant what I had said, even if I was not entirely certain those words were spoken in as much as they were felt.

Ian's will intensified, and I lost the will to breathe.

Suffused with the heat of a thousand suns, my body burned against his, feverish and flushed with a yearning I had long suppressed—a woman's want to love a man —and yet the amulet felt as if it were a diamond cut from a glacier. Its vacant chill frightened me. I felt so cold and alone, felt an emptiness sink into me, and by a force of will not my own, I removed it and placed it around Ian's neck all the while staring blindly into his eyes. When the gold chain settled itself against his flesh, he stared defiantly back into mine, and then suddenly— my lips forming breathless words—I began to recite a long forgotten memory:

> *Let me have possession of my soul.*
> *And of my spirit.*
> *And let me be true of voice with them…*
> *Wheresoever they may be.*

Those words…I felt as if I had spoken those words before, thousands of moons ago, in a daydream perhaps. At a time I could no longer place, they had rung like a death toll in my ears. I felt release in those words, felt the wounds healing, felt that I had found that which I had always assumed was forever lost to me. Forever fell away in those words.

Forever didn't seem so endless anymore.

What felt endless was Ian's passion. He looked down at my body and then smoothed his hand along my hip, his fingernails digging into my flesh as he traced the undulating lines of the winged serpent that bled angrily through my skin. "This is the dragon I saw in my dream," he said. "It was always you, Selena. It was always you." But I could just barely remember when that serpent had been born. It had uncoiled from hidden depths like a dark secret. Had torn its way through my flesh. All that was left to remember was the pain. I remember the sublime suffering of its birth, how the pain had been faint at first, deliciously soothing, almost seductive, and even though the serpent's venom had faded over the long years, I could remember it well enough to know when I felt that pain once again.

Through Ian's fingertips, I felt the loneliness clawing at me once more, but before I could push him away, the lightning sheared the darkness so violently that my instant reflex was to cling to him. Ian looked down at the amulet and then placed his hands upon my face as if he were coveting a memory not yet made. It was in that simple and tender gesture—trembling from his touch and rapt with ecstasy—that I felt love, a true, genuine love.

A love I could finally surrender to.

So I shifted my hips slightly beneath him. I gave in to him: allowed myself to want him, allowed myself to need him, allowed my body to rise up to meet him at the very threshold of his endurance...and of mine. I felt his body shudder with acceptance, a shudder defined by an undeniable purpose and power—a power only he and I could ever know or speak of—and with that power, he matched my thrust with his own and then breathed the affirmation I had so long waited to hear: "I love you too, Selena. How could I have ever resisted you?"

With those words, the room collapsed inward, the darkness—crumbling—fell away, and a saffron-colored haze rose up from the fire's exhalation. Slowly it moved, twisting and twirling through the blackness as it wrapped itself around Ian's words, attached itself to their shadows, altering their texture and intent.

The words became bits of fragmented thoughts. The thoughts, spanning all time and reason, filled my mind —*I love you Selena. In legion, we move*—and I remembered where it had all begun...at a time so long ago...when I shrank in despair at the night's cold dread hours and its thin empty shadows. Denied my dignity, I had swathed myself in hatred, bound myself to indifference. Love was beyond my grasp, and so it offered me nothing more than an unendurable emptiness. I used to marvel at how anyone could fare forth in that bitter darkness, alone, their souls laid bare, their minds twisted unnaturally under the torment of its burdening madness, and so I rejected it. I denounced it. I condemned love as utter foolishness: at worst, a heinous state of dementia, at best, a tedious fancy reserved for those of weaker will.

But now the hour had finally come. I could no longer just close my eyes and hope that it would go away. No longer blinded by the darkness, I did not fear the crea-tures lurking within the shadows nor did I fear the weapons that they uplifted against me. I felt neither the blade of longing nor the spear of despair.

I no longer felt unworthy.

I no longer felt beyond redemption.

Hatred had released me, set me stumbling to my knees at love's mercy. With Lucius, I could not restrain my fear, so I destroyed our love, and I had shed no tears over it, but now for the first time in my life, I feared it not. I no longer feared love and its abysmal depths. I feared only the parting it would inevitably bring, for within Ian's hands, he alone held the weapon that would be my undoing.

I could *feel* him—could *know* him. In each breath he took, I could taste my blood in his mouth. The thrust of his love was the coldest of blades. Running to and through my heart, it was sharper than any my own hand had ever wielded, and with that blade, I, for the first time, felt true salvation. I threw my arms open to the wind: a cruel untamed wind that had, in Ian's dream, set the sands of time against him. That wind drove hard at the windows and tore grave hollows into the darkness. The draperies thrashed about like lamenting specters, and the rain persisted, lashing at our bared flesh. Unrelenting, unabated, it offered ablutions to a worn and weary soul, and Ian's flesh, glossed over with rainwater, tasted of salt and soot. I could smell the distant sorrows of my ravaged homeland upon his brow.

Ian took me to the darkest place he knew, and I dreamt of home. It was then that I ascended.

Not *I*, the monster I had become…

Not *I*, the whore…

Not *I*, the slave, but a surreal, distorted sense of who

I once was and might have been. Floating with ease towards mysterious, forbidden places, I forgot myself and thought of Lucius. His voice, carried along by a rippling violet emptiness, reached out to me, and its dark infusion of undying ages, thoughts, and memories would comfort me on my long-winged flight through the void.

14

Salvation *and the Black River*

The mighty sun God, embarking upon its fiery descent, pierced the shifting clouds with blades forged of lightning and flame. A scarlet iridescence flooded the palms of my hands and glistened brilliantly in the blood still clinging, slick, to my fingers. Lost in the magnificence of the moment, I couldn't move, couldn't feel the presence of my own body. I could only stand there, silent and awestruck, my eyes fixed to the horizon just beyond the edge of the rocky precipice where I stood, into the abyss. There I gazed without regret into its vague and indistinguishable depths, and as I wrestled with an overwhelming sense of confusion and isolation, dense and luxurious threads of mist thrust sparkling white upward through the jagged rock beneath my feet and whirled in ribbons around me. The mist moved through my flesh, filled in the ruptured and empty spaces within me. I felt whole. I felt suffused with a sense of peace and tranquility the likes of which I had never known in all of my unnatural life. I knew it was time, and I was prepared. Had always been prepared. Time, like an acid, had eaten away at all my refusals, so I, who was once the inevitable, understood that there was no point resisting it. I took one slow step towards the edge, my foot casting sand and pebbles into the ravine. Their untimely descent into the abyss made no sound, but I could hear the river whispering. It was calling to me: "The rivers and the sea will always lead you home…" It was my father's voice, carried up to me upon an angry current of air. Lashing at my face, it rushed against me like the wind through the golden grasses of the steppe, lifting my hair high into the air, and I leant into it and closed my wearied eyes…

With my mind, I looked down upon that black river. How swiftly it travels upon its exalted course through vast empty caverns in the twilight. A river only the dead could presume to navigate, its chill swirling waters surge and tumble downwards, over and through charred mountains and jagged terrain as it carves its path into the wild, indescribably savage regions of the Cosmos. Indestructible and enduring, through mournful slopes, bleak and barren, it exhales its primeval vapors, releasing a vast wisdom to all who dare breathe in its will.

I would dare. I would not wait another eternity for death to bring me home. "O Black River of mourning, still and silent river of sorrow and hatred, your waters birth the end of the Universe, where mutable sunsets engulf your desolate shoreline. Yes, I see my fate beyond your horizon, just beyond my reach, and I will madly follow thee home." I breathed deeply, and it all became clear: I knew exactly where I was. The mortal world had finally released me. I knew that the blood on my hands was my own, that I had been loved and had given love in return, and in that knowledge, I knew the distance to the stars and all the secrets of the moon. In one fated breath, I knew the infinite sorrow of the world.

One leap. I knew then it would take but one—one leap of faith to free my soul, to wash away the centuries of blood and heartache, but my sword felt heavy in my hand, its worn blade gleaming in the approving gaze of the sun. It had been a part of me for so long, it had become me, so I took another deep, trembling breath, threw my arms out wide, and opened my eyes for the last time.

It was time to go home, but before I could commit, something startled me out of myself. My sword fell from my grasp, hit the rocks beneath my feet, and rang out a lament that would be heard across the barren chasms of time for centuries. A voice had called out to me: "Ilsebet," it begged from a distance that felt so close and yet so far away. "My beloved, Ilsebet," came again the echo shouted back from a time long abandoned, but it wasn't the words that pacified my will. It was that voice?

I recognized that voice, that gentle, deep voice ringing out from a memory—a memory so long lost and forgotten. It couldn't be? As I turned away from the void, the sun hit my eyes, casting a golden shimmer over everything…and within that golden shimmer, Lucius appeared before me, like a wish in a daydream. Not the mighty Kurgan warrior he had been born, the Egyptian God he had become, nor the Roman soldier I had once known, but a mortal man, the man I had once loved—still loved beyond all the bounds of reason.

His long, dark, and lustrous hair fell tussled in loose braids over broad shoulders. His garments—adorned with small golden plaques, like beads, but flat, ornamented with concentric circles—sparkled like jewels in the sun's vanishing rays, and the winged serpent emblazoned upon his flesh was no longer time worn and faded. It radiated a gilded vibrancy of translucent red ochre and indigo. He said my name again: *Ilsebet*, a name that had long ago taken leave of my memory, and when he told me that I was home, a tempest of emotions assailed me. This place, my name, his beauty, transcendent and overpowering, it was all much more than I could endure, so I flung myself at his feet, and with tears coursing down my face—tears so long restrained by the inconceivable degree of my hatred—I confessed my sins and pled for mercy. "I almost learned to hate you. I wanted to hate you. I have dreamt an endless solitude because I could never forget you. I love you, Lucius. I have always loved you, and I am so ashamed. I have witnessed the red blood of hatred consume the face of the moon, have willed it for my own idle fancy."

"No, Selena, do not weep." He knelt down, brushed my hair back over my shoulder, and embraced me with a powerful tenderness, his words filled with such compassion and love—sweet and poetic like the voice that had eternally lingered, haunting my memories of him. "I know that you love me. I have always known, and there is no cause for shame. It was your journey to make, and I was prepared and willing to take the risk, even though I knew it would take you away from me. I would have waited forever. Time would have known my heart for an eternity.

"Oh my sweet Selena, please stop crying now. You never lived a lie, and you never took a life that was not meant to be saved, including mine. My enduring love for you released me, and your impassioned hatred set me free, just as Ian's rage has set you free. There was no other way that it could have been, so it has always been.

"We are death, Selena. We are the light of Nehebkau, the harnesser of souls. Death is what we live and breathe. We were born dead. Not soulless. Not heartless. Cold and unaffected, perhaps, but not callous. Our existence is necessary artifice. For some we are mercy, and for others, we are vengeance. The deception is of their own invention, not ours. Our lives are merely the grim reflection of humanity's depravity, and we have died and been reborn a thousand times over by the time death calls us home from the abyss."

He smiled a sweet and comforting smile, pressed his lips firmly to mine, and sought my soul with his eyes—eyes that still shone with love. Eyes of the deepest mineral blue and crystallized amber—an ancient sea, captured forever within the golden resin of the Gods.

"Come now, Selena, it is time. In my arms, you will forget all the centuries of ruin and waste. You will forget yourself, life, and all torment. Love never changes. Our love has no beginning and no end. It is inexhaustible. Take your rest now from the shadows, let your love flow and console you. You have suffered your duty…you have bled for the Logos. Come now. We have all eternity to love one another. Come now to the black water where souls drown and the power of regret fades away. The ferryman awaits us, and he is slight of patience."

"But what of Sebastian?" I gasped in agony at the thought of him. "I cannot leave him."

"There is nothing more that you can do for him," Lucius affirmed in the gentle yet stern tack I adored. "Your time is over, Selena, his is just beginning. Your love has made him stronger than it was ever anticipated that he could be, and he will be, for as long as he must. And when his time comes, when he makes the choice to own his own soul, he will whisper the sacred words, and you will be here to embrace him. Do not worry for his soul, Selena. The amulet will shelter and bear the weight of its anguish. Come now…I have such magnificent sites to show you, flower petals and loveliness like you have never seen. It's time for us to just be."

He picked up my sword, took my hand, and then we moved down the sloping rock face towards the boat.

As Lucius flipped a coin to the ferryman, I remembered Homer's words: Witness this Earth. Witness this Heaven and the down-dropping waters of the Styx. I remembered closing my eyes as a child in Rome and whispering those words aloud as I envisioned this remarkable river of hate. Across the lands of the dead, it had called to me even then. I had seen it in my dreams often. Had gazed at my reflection in its waters, and yet even my mind's eye could not do justice to what lay before me. The splendor of the river was well beyond any conceivable dream—even an immortal's—and as I stood upon its coal-encrusted banks, I could hear my father's words gliding along its slick surface as it lapped at the oil-drenched shoreline: *The Rivers and the Sea will always lead you home.*

Its waters an echo of glistening obsidian, they reflected the violet hues of the sunset as Lucius and I cast away, into its murky depths, all of the hatred, shame, and regret of our mortal and immortal lives. Cleansed and purified, we would finally be able to move forth towards our destiny, always and forever together.

In the eons of light that passed, my thoughts often wandered back to the lonely painter who took up my sword. I imagined and hoped that his thoughts often wandered back to me.

Ian's rage would far surpass mine in its span and intensity. Through love, I had unleashed the savagery of a new terror, a terror whose manifest dread could never be imagined now or in all infinite time. For the first time in my life, I actually felt pity. I pitied all the lost and forsaken souls who would inevitably stumble across his path.

So Live, without Fear.

In legion we move, and we walk among you.

We are the Watchtowers.

We are the Horsemen.

We are the Leiche.

And I…am…Shadow.